# THE CACOUNA CAVES AND THE HIDDEN MURAL

Barbara Burgess

*The Cacouna Caves and the Hidden Mural*

Dedicated to Erika and Charles,
and my sister

The Cacouna Caves and the Hidden Mural
Copyright © 2018 by Barbara Burgess
All rights reserved.
First published in Canada
www.thecacounacaves.com

The painting featured on the cover is by Montreal artist
Graeme Ross

The use of any part of this publication reproduced, transmitted
in any form or by any means, electronic, mechanical,
photocopying, recording or otherwise stored in a retrieval
system, without the express written consent of the publisher,
is an infringement of the copyright law.
The descriptions of Cacouna, as well as the characters in the
novel, are based on my imagination and have no resemblance
to any real persons, places, or events.

The painting featured on the cover is by Montreal artist
Graeme Ross

## Contents

| | |
|---|---|
| FOREWORD | 9 |
| ONE: DEANNA | 13 |
| TWO: MATT | 23 |
| THREE: SARAH | 26 |
| FOUR: WASAWEG'S DIARY | 37 |
| FIVE: LE FLEUVE D'ARGENT (THE SILVER RIVER) | 49 |
| SIX: TOUCH NOT THE PAINTING | 57 |
| SEVEN: "THE LETTER KILLS, BUT THE SPIRIT GIVES LIFE" | 66 |
| EIGHT: KAKOUA-NAK ISLAND | 70 |
| NINE: WASAWEG AND MATTHIEU | 80 |
| TEN: THE SAINT JEAN BAPTISTE WEEKEND | 83 |
| ELEVEN: MOVING THE SACRED GLACIAL STONE | 96 |
| TWELVE: THE HIDDEN MURAL | 112 |
| THIRTEEN: SLIPPING BACK IN TIME | 123 |
| FOURTEEN: TRANSITIONS | 128 |
| FIFTEEN: DIANE | 134 |
| SIXTEEN: DELIVERANCE | 143 |
| SEVENTEEN: THE FORMIDABLE PROFESSOR | 151 |
| EIGHTEEN: DISCLOSURE | 155 |
| NINETEEN: END OF AN ERA | 171 |
| TWENTY: SACRIFICE | 177 |
| TWENTY-ONE: TIME STOOD STILL | 189 |

TWENTY-TWO: MOTHER………………………………...194
TWENTY-THREE: UNVEILED TREASURES…………200
TWENTY-FOUR: REBIRTH……………………………204
EPILOGUE: THE SILVER STARLIGHT………………..211
ACKNOWLEDGEMENTS………………………………217
ABOUT THE AUTHOR…………………………………221

He saw such brilliant coverings of a million trees and slowly flushing cheeks of the hills. All the dark spruce were now sprinkled with flashes of red, brown, yellow, vermillion, all so vivid, above the broad waters of the St. Lawrence River, which gleamed dark grey under the glowering clouds ... He had forgotten how wonderful the crisp cold air was in the autumn ...

—Paul Almond, author of the *Alford Saga*

# FOREWORD

While the novel includes some historical elements, it is a work of fiction, and I have altered the dates and geographical locations of certain elements in the narrative. Cacouna village did not exist yet in the 1600s when this story takes place, and to my knowledge, Cacouna Island was never invaded by the English. The archaeological site on the island is my own invention. However, historical evidence shows the indisputable presence of various indigenous peoples in the region.

I have consulted various researchers and carried out my own research, but I do not claim to be an expert on First Nations traditions, particularly the Wolastoqiyik (formerly known as "Maliseet") or the Mi'gmaq of the lower Saint Lawrence region. The Wolastoqiyik Wahsipekuk have a reserve in Cacouna; the region has long been a part of their hunting and fishing territory.

Today, the Gros-Cacouna marsh is a renowned ornithological site. About a dozen private residences are located on the north-eastern part of the island. The western end is occupied by the port of Gros-Cacouna.

In the sixteenth and seventeenth centuries, a number of European explorers, settlers and missionaries stopped in the Cacouna region. The crews renewed their supply of fresh drinking water from a freshwater source near the shore. Ships docked at a nearby natural cove to load barrels of salted fish to bring back to France. There were indeed many shipwrecks in the area.

Jacques Cartier makes mention of an island he sailed by. That island, l'île-Verte (Notre-Dame-des-Sept-

Douleurs), is located just northeast of Cacouna Island and lies close to it. So it can be assumed that Jacques Cartier may have seen Cacouna Island and possibly even visited it on one of his voyages along the Saint Lawrence River.

In 1690, Admiral William Phips of the Massachusetts Bay Colony commandeered a fleet of more than thirty British ships with two thousand soldiers. They first wreaked havoc on Acadia. In October 1690, on their way to Quebec City, which they hoped to conquer, a number of English boats showed up off the shores of Rivière-Ouelle, which is relatively close (seventy kilometres) to Cacouna. The inhabitants of Rivière-Ouelle managed to defend their parish, but the fleet went on to Quebec.

Some historians and writers with more expertise than I have on the subject have written about the foundation and history of the village in Cacouna. The first settlers to create the village were Acadian. After their expulsion from Acadia in 1755, thousands ended up leaving Acadia. The long journey from Grand-Pré to Cacouna on the Saint Lawrence River totals a distance of roughly eight hundred kilometres. One route from Acadia to Quebec followed the Madawaska River from the point of the Saint John River in Edmundston in New Brunswick and went to Lac Témiscouata, finishing with about eighty kilometres of portage in the region of Kamouraska right up to the Saint Lawrence River. (There were other routes as well, some of which were over a hundred and fifty kilometres in length with only fifteen kilometres of portage.)

During the New France era, some of the people living in the region were seasonal fishermen. The first group of Acadians arrived in Cacouna in 1758. Some of them stayed in the area, although others left in the following spring for central Quebec. The second group, directed by Michel Saindon, a notary and land surveyor, took the same route and arrived at Cacouna in 1764. More families settled in the area then, especially in Kamouraska, Saint-Jean-Port-Joli, Trois-Pistoles, and Rivière-Ouelle.

Some readers have asked me about the location of the caves. In fact, there are not three adjoining caves on Cacouna Island; rather, there is one cave long in use by the First Nations people. The reference to three caves is entirely my own invention. Furthermore, the locale is known today as Gros-Cacouna; however, it was referred to as Cacouna Island for many years, because, until the road to it was improved, it was often inaccessible during high tides. Some First Nations called it Kakoua-Nak Island. In the era of New France, some French called the region Cacona or Kakona. In this novel, in the sections narrated by Wasaweg, I call it Kakoua-Nak; elsewhere, I mainly refer to it as Cacouna Island.

*The Cacouna Caves and the Hidden Mural* is set in a part of the world—the lower Saint Lawrence region of Quebec, Canada—that is especially dear to my heart. My parents brought me to Cacouna for the first time when I was three months old. At that time we were living in Paris, France, so it was a pretty long trip!

In 1921, my British and Canadian ancestors first visited the Cacouna region of the Lower Saint Lawrence. My paternal grandparents were married in 1922 in Saint

Bartholomew's Anglican Church in nearby Rivière-du-Loup. They had fallen in love with a small cottage which my great aunt had bought earlier that year, in 1922, for her mother, my great-grandmother Sarah Jones. My great-great-grandfather Stephen Jones (who immigrated to North America in the nineteenth century, travelling by steamboat from England), planted the tiger lilies that still bloom today in the garden next to the cottage.

The cottage has now been in our family for a century. And so, while this book is a fantasy novel, it is also in part based on my own family's history and long association with Cacouna.

As a child, I used to swim in the cold Saint Lawrence River and lie in the sun on the sand. I went to the beach with my parents, sister, my grandmother, and other members of my father's family for picnics in the daytime and bonfires in the evening. Later, when I was older, I walked alone on the rocky beach lined with wild rose bushes. The sound of the waves was soothing. I would sit on the beach for long, "timeless" stretches of time. I often noticed a seal basking in the sun on a nearby rock. I especially loved one large boulder which my father, Charles, named "the mermaid rock." It looks out to the blue mountains on the North Shore across *le fleuve d'Argent*—the Silver River—our beautiful Saint Lawrence River.

— Barbara Burgess

## ONE: DEANNA

"Justin and I are taking off for the summer," Deanna announced from the front door. She slung off her knapsack and tossed it onto the carpet near the bottom of the stairway that led to her bedroom on the second floor. "He booked the loft of a quaint B&B—not far from Cacouna Island where he's got a job at that archaeological site I was telling you about."

Her father put his iPad on the table next to the sofa. "You started dating him how long ago? Less than three months."

She nodded, and swept her waist-long black hair behind her shoulders.

"You're rushing into it," he said. "You always do this, Deanna."

"Your father's right." Her mother paused. "Are you sure you're not jumping into things?"

"I'm nineteen. I can make my own choices. And I'll bring my books with me, get a head start on a major essay I'll have to write for an English literature course I enrolled in for the Fall semester. The cottage is in the countryside, so I won't have distractions." She was planning on writing about George MacDonald—the Scottish writer who had influenced J.R.R. Tolkien and C.S. Lewis.

Her mother eyed her skeptically. "Won't you be lonely with Justin away all day? And what exactly will he be doing?"

"He's going to work with seasoned archaeologists on site."

"But will it even be safe?" Her father frowned. "Justin will leave you alone at the cottage. We've already lost our son–we can't lose you too." He looked upset.

She knew what he was thinking. Her brother, Matthew, would have turned twenty last week. Their birthdays were just two days apart and they had always celebrated them together. A year ago, he'd gone missing–just vanished without a trace.

"I know," said Deanna. "I miss him too, all the time." She crossed the room and sat down beside her father on the sofa and hugged him, then hugged her mother as well. "But I'll be fine, don't worry. Sarah Beaumont, who runs the guesthouse, she'll be home all day, so I won't be alone. And the area's really peaceful and beautiful. I'll miss you both, but I'll Skype you every day–I won't seem far."

Her parents glanced at each other and smiled reluctantly. She knew she'd won the argument.

***

Justin and Deanna caught the early bus from downtown Montreal. At Sainte-Foy, on the outskirts of Quebec City, they scrambled onto the next bus and began the two-hour ride along Highway 132 to Rivière-du-Loup, a small city a few kilometres west of Cacouna village. Behind Deanna's sunglasses, her eyelids drooped from fatigue.

When she woke up, Justin was still sleeping, his head on her shoulder. Mesmerized, she looked out the window at the shimmering, silver river; it raced alongside the highway, and then danced away at the next curve. They were now about an hour from their destination and the landscape had totally changed. The softness of the atmosphere—the terrain and the billowing clouds—felt like the embrace of a mother. She perceived this maternal embrace to be the collective spirit of the land's first inhabitants, the First Nations, a fully embodied spirit pervading the trees, rolling through the sky on sacred clouds. It seemed to her that the spiritual devotion of all the souls who'd ever lived in rural Quebec had risen up and permeated those clouds.

The bus swerved around a corner and she glimpsed purplish blue, rolling mountains on the North Shore; the wide expanse of the Saint Lawrence River stretched toward the distant blue. The weight on her chest and the pain she had learned to live with—ever since Matthew had gone missing a year ago—lifted for a few moments. She inhaled the briny air—the seaweed-scented sky. She sensed her brother close by, as if she had returned home and he were about to greet her. She glued her face to the window. Tears poured down her cheeks. Was anyone watching on the bus? She didn't care.

They caught a taxi at the station in Rivière-du-Loup. Fifteen minutes later, they pulled into a pebbled driveway. Justin lugged their bags to the cottage steps and Sarah Beaumont, a short young woman with curly brown hair, greeted them at the front door of her guesthouse.

"Welcome!" She beamed at them. "You know, people around here use the kitchen door as the main entrance. You can come in that way from now on; it's around the back. So, let me give you guys a quick tour."

Inside, the cottage walls were painted white and the windowsills were royal blue. An old stone fireplace dominated the far end of the living room. A colourful hooked rug lay on the wooden floor. Dark wood beams supported a low ceiling. Bookshelves lined one wall.

"That's my bedroom," Sarah said, pointing to a room off the living room. "You must be tired from your trip. I'll make tea. You can unpack and settle in upstairs. You've got to be careful on the ladder to the loft. Don't slip."

A few hours later, they were settled in their bedroom for the night, lying under the wide woolen blankets, alone with each other and away from all the pressures of the city and stresses of the past year.

Deanna was entranced by the rustic guesthouse and its surroundings. A cast-iron woodstove filled one corner of the cozy yellow kitchen. Through the kitchen window she could see a dilapidated barn and a long lawn and fenced-in garden. A gazebo in the distant woods perched near a cliff and overlooked the Saint Lawrence River.

Sarah's father had died of cancer two years earlier, three days shy of his fifty-second birthday. Her mother hadn't had enough money to pay for property taxes and so, rather than sell the place, they had decided to convert the three-hundred-year-old cottage into a bed and breakfast. While Helen was away taking an intensive Business Management course over the summer, Sarah was running the guesthouse by herself. She was just two years older than Deanna and they hit it off immediately. Whenever Justin was around, she gave them a lot of space and appeared only to offer a fresh cup of tea or a meal. She would retire to the kitchen where she could be heard clicking away on her computer at a corner table.

They had been in Cacouna for a couple of weeks. It was a sunny day and Justin had left for work. Deanna stood outside on the porch beneath the sloping tin roof. She looked out at the low-lying mountains across the river. She felt drawn to cross the water and reach their distant blue slopes.

The kitchen door opened and Sarah joined her on the veranda. "The North Shore mountains are beautiful, eh? When you take a ferry across and get to the other side, you realize, of course, that the blue mountains aren't blue—it's just an illusion created by the distance."

"How wide is the river from here to the other side?"

"I'd say about twenty-five kilometres. The ferry ride's amazing. You can often see beluga whales from the deck. If you do go, bring binoculars."

Sarah's neighbour, twenty-five-year-old Pierre—a tanned man with angular features and kind eyes—appeared on his porch and called out over the lawn. "You guys want to join me on a walk? My pick-up's in the garage for the day. I'm going to walk along the highway past the village, then come back by the beach."

"I've got tons to do around here today," Sarah yelled back. "But *she's* free!" She pointed at Deanna.

"I'll meet you near the driveway in five minutes. Put on a good pair of walking shoes and a sun hat for the beach." He darted back inside.

"Trying to get me out of the house, are you?"

"Love your company, but you can't sit around reading all day, especially when it's this nice outside. You *have* to keep moving."

Deanna nodded. "You mean I have to keep moving on with my life, don't you? Even if my brother doesn't come back … "

Sarah draped her arm around the young woman's shoulder. "I know a bit what you're going through. My mom and I knew Daddy wasn't going to make it, but you can never really be prepared, can you? It must have been much harder for you. You had no warning. I found it helped to keep busy."

As they began walking, Deanna asked Pierre if, after he finished his errands in the village, they could cross over to Cacouna Island and surprise Justin—these days he was working near the beach on the northern part of the island.

"It's too far to walk from here. And the beach on the northern half of the island would be completely covered by water, because the tide is high around noon today. We can go another day at low tide and by car."

"Sure, I'd love that."

"In the old days, you know, you couldn't access the island at all during high tides in spring and autumn, except by boat. Then a few years ago, they raised the causeway that the road is paved over. Doing so created a dam and now the river doesn't flood the road anymore. You can drive there any time of year."

"So those are just private residences over there, right?"

"Yup. Although in the past, farmers lived on it all year round. Way back in 1898, an idealistic French priest called Father Louis Stevenart rented a farmhouse on the island. Created an institution that he called 'le Prado' modeled on something similar in France. He gathered a dozen orphans from Holland, France, and Belgium and sailed from Europe. Took nine weeks to reach Canada by boat. The priest tried growing potatoes and raising geese on Cacouna Island. The mission didn't last the winter."

"Poor orphans."

"Well, they all got placed in homes on the mainland. Actually, I'm a descendant of one of those boys."

She gave him a quick glance. "Wow! What a story! And the name—Cacouna Island? That's not English or French. What language is it?"

"The indigenous people called the island *Kakoua-Nak*, 'land of the porcupine.'"

"Oh, I get it. It looks like a porcupine from a distance! How clever!" Deanna paused. "And does the road go right across the island?"

"No. It doesn't reach the north-western half. You'd have to park by the last private house and hike along the far beach quite a ways to get near where Justin's working. There's no public access."

"Oh, so that's why Justin said a boat picks him and the team up and drops them off near the dig. I never asked him why. So it's because of the tides. I guess I haven't been paying too much attention to his work. I've been distracted."

"The motorboat's only used by the people working the site. No one else is allowed in that area. I have a cousin who owns a cottage on the island, so no one really objects if I wander about. We'll have to time it so we go when the tide is low; otherwise, it's impossible to walk on the beach—it's completely submerged in water, you see. I'll take you to the dig, promise, when my pick-up's out of the garage, but I warn you, be prepared for a very long walk on extremely rocky terrain." He gave her a dubious look.

"Yah, yah. I know you're thinking—City Girl. But really, I work out at the gym and I walk home from McGill University five times a week."

"Oh. That's a long walk. You live in Westmount, right? Justin told me. He showed me a photo of you and him standing in front of your parents' house. You must have quite the view of Montreal."

"Yes. But nothing compared to this breathtaking scenery."

Just past Cacouna village, Jean Prevost had converted his huge, red-roofed barn into an antique shop. At the back of the store, Pierre pulled a faded green book off a bookshelf. It had gold lettering on the cover: *Cacouna's History* by Jane Scott. He glanced at the copyright page.

"Second Edition, 1910," the antiquarian said over his shoulder. He had followed him and wanted to chat. "Scott wrote it over a century ago."

"It could be useful," Pierre mused. "In my spare time, I'm building a website about the history of Cacouna. But ... fifty dollars!" He wavered. He worked as a landscaper from spring to autumn and spent most of the winter unable to work because of the snow.

Deanna silently approached behind them. "Let me buy it for you."

"No, no. It's too much. I can't accept."

"It's no problem, Pierre. Consider it a contribution to your website. I'll be visiting it, you can be sure."

"Okay ... very generous. Thank you." He glanced admiringly at her as they walked toward the counter. Who could guess that this tall young woman, dressed in faded jeans and a bright red tank top, was the daughter of a high-ranking Canadian politician? Sarah had told him that Deanna was from a prestigious family and that her brother had gone missing one year ago. Pierre ruminated: *No matter how wealthy and well-placed you are, material prosperity and status don't guarantee happiness in life.* He snuck another look at her as she passed Jean a hundred-dollar bill over the counter. Her black hair accentuated her blue eyes, in which lingered a deep sadness.

They waved goodbye to the antiquarian and started back, walking along the main road and skirting the Cacouna Golf Course. Along the way, Deanna opened up to Pierre about her missing brother and even stopped to show him a photo of Matthew on her iPhone. Just past the village post office, they turned onto Rue du Quai and descended the steep asphalt road to Rue de la Grève, which paralleled the beach. A one-storey building stood near the corner and overlooked the water. A sign read: Première Nation Wolastoqiyik Wahsipekuk.

Pierre pushed open the door and stepped in.

"Hello?" He called out.

No one answered.

"Anyone here who can help us?" He waited for a few moments and started to leave.

A voice called out: "*Un moment, s'il vous plaît.*" (Just a moment, please.)

A young man, in his early twenties, emerged from the back of a dimly lit room. His dark brown eyes smiled warmly at them over the pile of boxes he held in his arms. Deanna stared at him—a stunned look in her eyes.

"Dream catchers," he said. "Everyone loves them—you know—they wash away bad dreams and clear the way for good ones. A new shipment arrived in time for Saint Jean Baptiste Day." He unloaded the boxes on the front counter. "Lots of people visit over the holiday. Hey! Why not join us? We'll make a bonfire on the beach and we'll party to live music performed by locals."

"Love to!" said Pierre. He extended his hand. "I'm Pierre, this is Deanna, and you're—?"

"Matt."

That was the last thing Deanna heard before her knees buckled and she fell unconscious.

## TWO: MATT

When she regained consciousness, Deanna was lying on a sofa. Pierre lightly pressed a cold, damp washcloth against her forehead. She opened her eyes briefly, then closed them again and listened to him talking with the young man.

"She's ill?" Matt was asking. His voice had a worried tone. "She seemed fine when she walked in with you. I'll call 911!"

"I think she'll be okay in a few minutes."

"What's happened?"

"I imagine she's in shock." Pierre helped Deanna sit up; some colour was returning to her face but she kept her eyes closed. "Her brother Matthew went missing a year ago. She showed me his photograph when we were walking earlier. You're the spitting image of him. I think when you mentioned your name, coincidentally the same as his, it must have been too much for her—brought it all up."

"How devastating for their family."

"Is there any chance you could be related to Matthew Aynsworth? Do you have relatives in Montreal?"

"None. My lineage in Cacouna goes back more than three hundred years. Long before the village was founded, my father's ancestor, Matthieu Landry, arrived from France. Matthieu married a Mi'gmaq woman and settled here. The Landrys never left the region. My mum, Danielle, is mostly Wolastoqiyik—that part of the family moved to Cacouna in the 1800s—with some Mi'gmaq ancestry from New Brunswick as well."

"When did your Landry ancestor arrive from France?"

"It was 1683. Matthieu Landry was a sea captain. The river is beautiful, but terrible, too—we've had countless shipwrecks along this stretch of the Saint Lawrence River. The wooden sailing ships, blown off course by gale winds, got easily punctured and sunk by reefs and boulders in shallow waters. So many sea graves, marked and unmarked …" His words trailed off. "Anyway, the French merchant vessel washed ashore near Cacouna Island. At the time, over three hundred years ago, a small Mi'gmaq community had been living on the island for some years. The sea captain, my ancestor, fell in love with Wasaweg—sister to the healer in the clan. Matthieu remained on the island, and he and Wasaweg had a daughter, Isabelle, and then a son, Matthis. The tradition in our family has been, for over three centuries, to name each eldest son 'Matthieu' after our French forefather."

"Ah, that explains all the variations on your name." Pierre chuckled.

"Yes. But it's a tragic story. Matthieu Landry went missing in 1690, after they'd been married for seven years, so Wasaweg had to bring up the children alone. A long time ago, a little girl discovered Wasaweg's journal in the attic of a summerhouse in Cacouna. I have it here. I confess I've only leafed through the diary. You guys can borrow it if you like."

"Thank you."

Deanna opened her eyes.

"Do you think you're ready to head back to the cottage?" Pierre asked.

She nodded.

"Could you arrange a taxi for us?" he asked Matt.

"No, no! I'll drive you myself. I insist. It's the least I can do when a customer faints in my store!"

Right before they left, Deanna saw him hand over an old-looking manuscript that she knew had to be Wasaweg's diary.

"Cool place. Rustic. Not all modernized like some houses," said Matt as he pulled into the driveway. "I haven't been here in ages."

"Sarah Beaumont's guesthouse," said Pierre.

"So she runs it now as a B&B? I'm glad they didn't sell the cottage after her dad died. Sarah and I went to high school together, you know, but I haven't seen her much since Mr. Beaumont died. Too bad. He was too young. I should visit her some time." He turned his head and said to Deanna, who was in the back seat, "I didn't mean to give you a shock. You're sure you're okay now?"

"No worries. It wasn't your fault." She studied his face. *He and my brother could be identical twins. How bizarre.*

After the car drove away and went around the bend, she burst into tears.

## THREE: SARAH

The next morning, Sarah plunked the teapot on the dining room table, lifted off the tea cozy, and re-filled two cups. Sunlight streamed through the bay window and the blue mountains loomed across the river. Justin was still sleeping in the loft bedroom—it was Sunday and his only day off.

Deanna stirred the sugar into her teacup thoughtfully. "I felt quite unnerved, meeting Matt like that at the Wolastoqiyik Wahsipekuk First Nation Centre yesterday. If I didn't know better, I'd think he and my brother were twins."

"I'm so sorry you got shocked—it's awful, what you've had to go through this past year. I can't imagine it."

"What can we do? Life's like that sometimes." Deanna shrugged. "I'd heard everyone has a look-alike *somewhere* in the world—a doppelganger. So strange that I come face to face with a guy who's the spitting image of my missing brother. Felt like a knife in my gut."

"Do you want to talk about Matthew?"

Deanna stared into space. "You'll think I'm crazy."

"Try me. You'd be surprised."

"I've never told anyone the full story, not even my parents. They'd freak out that I'm delusional. They think maybe he wanted to run away from our family and the city. He never fit into the Westmount crowd, you know. He often talked about wanting to visit Asia, see other cultures, other continents. Then, a year ago, he just disappeared. My parents are terrified something horrible happened to him. I don't know where he went, but I—I saw him go, Sarah. And I know what I saw, although I still can't believe it. It defies reason. The worst of it is, I can't tell anyone."

"So tell me. I'll be discrete."

Deanna glanced around to make sure no one else was nearby. "My mom's on the board at the Montreal Museum of Fine Arts. Our family had gone to the opening night of an exhibit of late seventeenth-century portraits of explorers who left France for the New World. No one else remained in the exhibition hall. Everyone had left for the wine and cheese party—it was the *vernissage.* Only Matthew and I were left standing in that wing of the gallery. He didn't want to leave. I told him we were late for the reception, but he kept staring at this painting. He wouldn't budge. He must have stood in front of it for ten minutes, his feet glued to the floor. Then he reached out and touched the picture frame—and … he vanished."

Sarah was quiet.

"I mean—he *vanished*, Sarah! Into thin air! One moment he was standing beside me in the Montreal Museum of Fine Arts, the next minute—space."

Sarah pondered. "What was the title of the painting?"

"*Two European explorers on the deck of an old French sailing ship.* Artist unknown."

"Did it by chance mention the explorers' names?"

"Yes, in smaller print, below the first caption, it read: 'Sieur Charles de Beaumont and Captain Matthieu Landry Set Forth for New France'."

Sarah stood up and paced around the living room for a few minutes. Then she sat down at the table and took Deanna's hands in her own. "Have you ever wondered why you ended up in Cacouna at my B&B?"

"No, should I? All I know is Justin was surfing online and found your website. He liked the pictures of the cottage—and you."

"Yes, but why *my* B&B? Think, Deanna. What's my name?"

"Sarah."

"My full name."

"Sarah Beaumont. Oh!"

"I've researched our family ancestry thoroughly—it's a passion of mine—and discovered that Charles de Beaumont, the son of the French king's financial advisor, was my distant ancestor. He sailed here as a young man in 1666 to represent a group of French merchants. In 1683, on a second trip to New France, he hired a sea captain—Matthieu Landry. Off Cacouna Island, a gale arose and the ship crashed into a reef. The boat got totaled."

"Charles de Beaumont clearly survived; you're living proof—his descendant. What about the sea captain, how did he survive the shipwreck?"

"After Beaumont and a handful of his men swam ashore, Matthieu Landry, who couldn't swim, clung on to the ship's hull for hours. It was his good luck that the river carried him to the mainland where Jesuit priests rescued him. Beaumont, who was not a nice man, if I might add, heard that the sea captain had survived, and he placed a bounty on his head. He falsely claimed that Landry had deliberately steered the ship into the reef. Beaumont wanted to smear his name and land him in a French prison or worse—have him executed."

"That's horrible! Why would Beaumont make up such a story?"

"Years later Landry confided to his wife that aboard the ship, he had caught Charles de Beaumont red-handed with the French king's stolen jewels. Beaumont had hidden a huge ruby, an emerald, and three diamonds inside a strongbox tucked away in his cabin. Matthieu Landry had confronted him. That was why the 'nobleman' wished to discredit and silence him. So, to escape, Matthieu Landry fled to Cacouna Island and went into hiding."

"What happened to Charles de Beaumont?"

"Rather ironically, the king granted him a large tract of land, a *seigneurie*, near Quebec City. The French king had no idea that his own finance minister's son had orchestrated the theft of French royal jewels."

"Outrageous! Did they ever recover the jewels from the shipwreck?"

"No clue. But I do know that Charles de Beaumont became the richest businessman in New France in his day. So I suspect that he got them out of the safe and slipped them in his satchel before he swam to shore."

Deanna raised her eyebrows.

"I know. You're wondering why our cottage is this dilapidated if I'm the descendant of a wealthy landowner. Well, long story short, I'm the direct descendent of Bernard Beaumont, Sieur Charles' youngest son, who hated his father's ruthless tactics. At sixteen, he took off from home and travelled from Quebec City to this region to settle here. When Wasaweg's brother approached him, Bernard sold him part of the land. He befriended Lentug's family—his sister Wasaweg and her two children—and helped them build on the property."

"A good neighbour."

"Yes. And actually, Bernard married into their family, when Isabelle turned eighteen. He had fallen in love with her—Matthieu's and Wasaweg's only daughter. After they married, the two adjoining properties merged again. That's why my plot of land is so big, even though Daddy had to sell that field over there to make ends meet." Sarah pointed to the left.

"How ironic! Beaumont's rebellious son Bernard marries the daughter of the man who is on his 'wanted' list."

"Yes, but Matthieu Landry, Isabelle's father, had already been missing for more than a decade by the time she got married. It's quite romantic." She smiled. "Isabelle and Bernard, like Wasaweg and Matthieu before them, married for love, not for family connections. Their daughter married a man from Rivière-du-Loup, Fabien Gauthier, and they had kids, and so on and so on. *Eh bien*, the result is me!"

"Wow! What a story. So you're part French and part First Nation, way back."

"I am."

"Like Matt, the man I was telling you about, whom we met at the First Nation Centre yesterday. I think you guys know each other?"

"Yes, Matt and I figured out that we are distantly related. We used to hang out in the village, but I haven't seen him since I graduated from high school." Sarah smiled. "I should give him a phone call."

"Funny, he said the exact same thing." Deanna paused. "Do you mind my asking why you still carry the Beaumont name? I mean, Isabelle's daughter married that guy, Fabien Gauthier, you said. Wouldn't she have changed her last name after marriage?"

"No. You see, we have a custom that any woman in our family who gets married must retain the Beaumont surname. And the husband of the eldest daughter *must* live on this property," she continued. "It's a tradition established by Isabelle Landry after her marriage with Bernard Beaumont." But she didn't express the last part of her thought ... *and must live on this property ... near the sacred stone in the garden.*

"Don't you think it's a bit odd? I mean, I meet you, and you're related to Charles de Beaumont, whose portrait my brother was staring at the night he disappeared. And then I meet Matt Landry, who looks identical to my brother. He even shares the same first name!"

"Perhaps it's not a coincidence," said Sarah softly.

"Maybe not. But in any case, nothing will bring *my* Matthew back. Mum still hopes he's alive, living under another identity, maybe in South America." The muscles around Deanna's mouth grew tight as she fought to keep herself from crying.

Sarah reached out and squeezed her hand. "It must be awful."

"It's worse to be tortured by hope, because when someone goes missing, you never know—you always live in uncertainty. One day I hope he's coming back, the next day I'm sure I'll never see him again, and then sometimes I think I see him in a crowd, or on Mount Royal when I'm walking back from school. And the dreams—they're the worst. I wake up thinking he's still with us, but he's gone. Daddy's given up. He believes Matthew's dead. Maybe that's his way of dealing with it. … Can you pass the Kleenex?"

"Sure. Wanna talk about something else?"

Deanna nodded and blew her nose. "Do you know anything more about Matthieu Landry's disappearance? Yesterday, Matt loaned us Wasawcg's diary. I started reading it last night. Pierre was nice enough to let me take a look at it first. Said he's too busy to read, but I think he wants me to keep my mind busy." She reached into her knapsack, pulled out an old manuscript bound by tattered red cloth, and placed it on the table next to the teapot. "I devoured the first chapter. I think it must have been so hard for Wasaweg, not knowing if her husband was missing or dead, and also having to raise their two children alone."

Sarah thought, *Deanna hasn't changed the subject at all. But it must help her to know that she's not the only one in the world who's had to go through such personal agony.* "Well, I do know that they spent seven happy years together on Cacouna Island. Maybe you should focus on the good times they shared ... I heard that it was smack in the middle of their move to the mainland that he disappeared."

"Kind of like what happened to my brother. One moment he was there, the next moment he vanished."

"Yah, I guess so. I don't really know the full story. I heard snippets from my grandmother, and I was very little. Something about him not being a good swimmer."

"So no one ever saw him again?"

"No. Later on, her children encouraged Wasaweg to remarry, but she didn't. For years, she'd sit at the lookout—" Sarah pointed to a gazebo visible through the kitchen window, about twenty metres from the house. "For hours and hours every day she'd stare at the Saint Lawrence River, from low tide to high tide and high tide to low tide ..."

"Hoping her husband would come back?"

Sarah nodded. "At night, she worked on her weaving. Maybe it was therapeutic, the way some novelists write when they want to keep their minds occupied or channel their emotions about some chronic heartache." She cleared her throat, realizing she'd revealed too much about her own motivation for spending hours writing. "Anyway, Grandma told me it took Wasaweg a decade to complete the mat that she wove from cedar bark, grasses, and bulrushes."

"*A decade?*"

"Yes. You'll understand when you see the weaving. It's a work of art—it should be in a museum, really, but she stipulated that she wanted it kept in the family. It hangs over the doorway just inside the barn. I should really move it into the cottage to give it prominence, but I kind of like keeping it secret. Anyway, if you're curious, the key to the barn is on the stone mantelpiece over the fireplace." Sarah smiled and stood up. "I'll go make some coffee and toast. I hear Justin stirring in the loft. Must be breakfast time." She retreated into the kitchen.

Justin came down the ladder in his pyjamas and kissed Deanna. "Nice to sleep in. Got any plans for today?"

"I started Wasaweg's diary last night. I think I'll spend the day reading."

"I'm going to Rivière-du-Loup. Pierre's dropping me off and I'll walk back. You'll have the place to yourself —it's Sarah's day off and she's going out too."

After both had left, Deanna picked up the manuscript and headed for the hammock that hung between two old apple trees in the garden. *Nothing like a hammock and a good book—it doesn't get much better.*

But an hour later, Deanna still couldn't settle. She left the journal swinging in the green netting and wandered back into the kitchen for a snack. She checked her email and thought of phoning her parents, but didn't. Restless, she grabbed the key from above the fireplace and strode across the lawn to the barn.

The padlock, blackened and rusted with age, didn't open at first. Finally, the key turned, and Deanna pushed hard against the heavy, dark green door and entered. A couple of the shingles had slipped off the roof, leaving wide cracks through which the pale blue sky shone.

A chipmunk squealed at her as it raced across the floor. "Hey Chippie!" she called out. "Sorry to intrude. Guess you think this is your home, eh?" It darted into a hole in the wall.

Bunk beds, once painted bright yellow but now faded, stood in disuse in the far corner—draped with cobwebs. Nearby, a khaki-green travel trunk was tucked away, with three bags of lime for whitewashing beside it. *Looks like this place could do with a couple of coats of paint. Sarah hinted she was hard up for money and doesn't get many guests. I wonder why she and her mom don't try and get the property recognized as a Canadian heritage site. They could receive funding to renovate the buildings. I'll ask Daddy if we can help her.*

Then she saw it—the one bright spot inside the dilapidated building: protected by glass, Wasaweg's huge weaving hung over the doorway. So many happy scenes: Matthieu and Wasaweg holding hands, sitting on an enormous, flat grey rock rimmed with rose bushes and bright red rosehips. The Big Dipper sparkled over the pair of lovers—brilliant silver stars made from the silvery white tips of porcupine quills that the artist had embedded in an azure sky. *God, Wasaweg was gorgeous with her long black hair, dark eyes, and her mouth smiling tenderly at her husband. Why do the Landry men—old and modern—all look exactly like my brother?* Anger suddenly choked her. *I thought by coming to Cacouna I'd get away from it all, at least for a couple of months.* Tears streamed down her face. She sat down on the trunk and sank her head in her hands, crying uncontrollably. *I would do anything to see Matthew again.*

When she looked up, she saw—in the lower right corner of the weaving—a lone seal on a rock in the foreground. She stood up and paced the barn to look at it from different angles. The seal's gaze followed her wherever she moved, his eyes almost human. It had a small eight-point star on its forehead.

She returned to the garden and flopped into the hammock. She flipped the journal open to the middle and read aloud a poem Wasaweg had written.

> *Like a flame, you have risen*
> *So high in the sky I cannot see you,*
> *Yet I see your glory spread throughout*
> *The soft, rose-gold clouds*
> *On Kakoua-Nak Island.*

# FOUR: WASAWEG'S DIARY

At noon the next day, Sarah returned from a brisk walk to find Deanna rocking listlessly in Grandpa Beaumont's pine rocking chair in the living room. "You don't want to go for a walk? It's lovely and crisp out."

"Too chilly. I can't believe it's summer. It's only twelve degrees!"

"The weather can turn on a dime here. One moment it's cold and foggy and next minute—clear, sunny skies. Got any plans? Are you going to work on your paper on George MacDonald?"

"Nope. I've got massive writer's block today. I think I'll just laze around in front of the fireplace and try and stay warm. I called Pierre earlier for a walk, but he's over by some mansion creating a fancy-schmancy garden for some rich lady. Everyone's busy."

"Hey, did Pierre ever tell you about the rock in my backyard?" Sarah pointed out the window to the large, flat grey rock in the middle of the back lawn. *I've got to distract her from her bummed out mood,* she thought.

"No, he didn't. Why, is it special?" Deanna perked up.

"A year ago, this geologist, Bernadette, visited our guesthouse. She told me she had heard an intriguing First Nations tale about an ancient glacial rock that had landed, thousands of years before, on Cacouna Island—a gift from the Great Spirit, the legend said. The Mi'gmaq treated it as a holy stone—they believed it brought blessings, kept them safe, and served as a portal to other worlds and dimensions. Bernadette wanted to check out the story, because often myths hold kernels of truth. She explained the scientific basis to the legend. When the glaciers thawed over ten thousand years ago, the melting ice left the rock on the island. After the Ice Age, when the waters receded, the land gradually became covered with vegetation. A forest sprang up around the rock."

"But how does that relate to the rock in your garden?"

"Patience, Deanna. It's a long story, and, since you have nothing better to do, I'm here to entertain you." Sarah laughed. "So anyway, Bernadette had heard several local accounts of a strange tale ... During the New France era, the First Nations people who were then living on Cacouna Island held a feast and great ceremony to shift the holy rock off their island. Their leader, Lentug, a healer and visionary, had dreamed they were about to be invaded by the English and had decided they must leave and move the sacred stone with them. He was Wasaweg's brother."

"Wasaweg—your ancestor!" Deanna exclaimed.

"Yes. So this is the story behind how my family ended up settling here."

"And that's the rock?" Deanna looked out the window at it, perplexed and excited. "How exciting! But it would be impossible to move it," she mused. "It's enormous. I mean, isn't Cacouna Island like five kilometres away? How on earth could they transport that glacial rock all the way to your garden?"

"Dunno. It can't be explained by science. The people living on the island certainly couldn't have shifted it to this location by water; it weighs a ton and would have sunk a canoe. All I know is that when Bernadette analyzed the rock in our garden, she found traces that are an exact match to chips of rock she found in a depression on Cacouna Island, right where the rock would have originally stood according to legend. And she said it definitely dates back to the last Ice Age."

"I bet Wasaweg writes about it in her diary. I should keep reading."

Deanna went out to the lawn and lay in the hammock between the two gnarly apple trees. It was windy, and she tucked a woolen blanket around her body and swung in the green netting. She glanced at the huge glacial rock. *What a mystery*, she mused. *Now, where was I?* She reopened the manuscript and began to read Wasaweg's words. As she did, a hawk soared over a spindly spruce tree that towered over the barn. The bird flew so high, it looked like a tiny leaf blowing upward and away in the sky.

***

### *Wasaweg's Journal*

*Kakoua-Nak Island, seventeenth century*

*Here below, with accompanying drawings, is my account of the Mi'gmaq of this area and beyond. My mother told me that long before French explorers stumbled upon its existence, many Mi'gmaq families were living in an area between Rivière-du-Loup and Métis-sur-Mer. Their homes bordered the southern banks of the Saint*

Lawrence River. The South Shore stretched over many hundreds of kilometres and extended toward the interior to the highlands. All this made up a small part of the vast territory occupied by our Mi'gmaq ancestors, who, along with the neighbouring Wolastoqiyik nation, formed a large branch of the Algonquian family.

    Our people inhabited the entire region from here in Cacouna to the tip of the Gaspé Peninsula, between the St. Lawrence River and the shores of Nova Scotia, including all the islands near these shores. The Mi'gmaq were the undisputed masters of this land. Their territory was rich and fertile, the land near the Saint Lawrence especially so. The woods swarmed with moose, deer, caribou, bear, hare, and partridge. Rivers and lakes were abundant with beaver, trout, eel, seal, and salmon. Myriad water birds flocked to the banks of the river. The forest was full of pine, maple, and birch to build canoes. Our Mi'gmaq are hardworking, intelligent, and distant from the fierce peoples of the south and west. We enjoyed tranquility among the nations. At peace with each other and far from any enemies, we spent our lives in contentment and ease, happy in Nature.

    Canoe construction began when the sap flowed through the birch trees' veins and it was easier to peel the birch bark. So, every spring, young men went into the forests to get large strips of bark from the giant birch trees.

    Children enjoyed the warmth and brightness after the long, dark winter. Before the wigwam doors, children played on the grass; and women and girls braided roots, stitched moccasins, using matachias—little ornaments of beads, porcupine quills, or braided *strings—to decorate the cradles that swung from the tree branches. In the village fields, men built cedar canoes. Mothers gently pushed the tiny cradles in which their infants rested. The difficulties of the winter were forgotten, the future was fortunately concealed, and the thought of experiencing trouble never entered anyone's mind. Everyone worked quietly, sitting and talking in low tones about their dreams and reveries.*

*We used to meet once a year during springtime at the Bay of Bic to rest from our labours and spend a few weeks together. Then we would go our separate ways along the river's shore. But after the terrible spring massacre at Bic in 1534, some of our family's ancestors stopped going to the big yearly reunions, and instead simply celebrated together at a small village hidden away on Cacouna Island where they had set up their conical birch-bark-covered homes. The children loved to go berry picking and then swim in the cold river. For Great River Mijioqon had been freed of ice at last by the warm sun and high spring tides, and everything appeared beautiful and reborn. The soft, light-green foliage of the budding aspens, birch and cherry trees mixed with the dark-coloured evergreens—spruce and fir and cedar and pine.*

*From the village centre, pathways zigzagged in different directions toward the woods and hills. Village life was calm and happy, and the hours passed peacefully.*

On one such day in June, four years after Matthieu and I had got married, the English-speaking foreigner arrived on the island. My husband found her lying on the beach. He led her to our home and asked me to take care of her. She was bewildered during her first days with us. Matthieu thought she might have suffered a head injury. Within a few weeks, she settled into our life and seemed happy—at least, she expressed no wish to leave the island. She told us her name was Diane. (My daughter called her "Sky Eyes" because of her blue eyes.) She didn't tell us anything about her past or her family, if she had any relatives. She stayed with our family for three years. She soon became close friends with Émilie, the young French novice from the nearby convent on the mainland, who had begun living with us right after Matthieu and I got married, because her Mother Superior threw her out into the cold.

Diane was a little younger than Émilie, and her wigwam was closer to ours. She helped watch over our children whenever we canoed to the mainland to trade with the French who needed our help, because they didn't know the lay of the land very well. In return, we asked for books from the traders. Diane taught us her language and I became literate. So now I could not only speak French, which Mathieu had taught me, I could read and write both English and French too. That was when I began writing this journal. Diane encouraged me to record the stories that our people, the First People, have passed down orally for generations. She learned our language quickly, too. I remember that after I taught her that *buseneg* meant "Let us take a journey over water by canoe", she said, "A whole sentence in one word? Fantastic!"

Life was peaceful, but three years after Diane joined us, the English began to make inroads into the region. We heard rumours that a great fleet of more than thirty ships was being assembled by Admiral Phips. He was the governor of the Massachusetts Colony. They attacked Port Royal, the capital of Acadia. We got nervous. We feared it was only a matter of time before they'd try to take over the entire countryside as they moved toward the large settlement at Quebec.

"You've got to stand up for your rights," Diane warned us. "Europeans, French and English alike, plan to steal *Mi'gma'gi*—land of the Mi'gmaq. Wasaweg, you're a great leader in your community. Don't let this happen. Don't allow them to venture onto the island. They'll try to lure your community with metals and *pugtaw,* fire-water, or alcohol as my people call it. Later, they'll offer you treaties. All you'll ever receive from them will be broken promises, abuse, massacres, and diseases. You'll lose your land, homes, and freedom."

"How do you know? You're sure?" asked six-year-old Isabelle, who had been listening to our conversation while I braided her hair.

"Alas, I've had strange dreams about what will happen to this beautiful land and its inhabitants in the future," Diane answered.

We Mi'gmaq understand dream-visions, but the notion of future time is inherently foreign. Isabelle piped up, "What's 'future,' Diane? You often talk about what might happen in future. You worry too much! Uncle Lentug says that the water which will flow toward us from the source, the water that moves directly past us, and the stream that has already passed beyond us, are not three kinds of water. It's all the same water."

Diane burst into laughter and patted her on the head. "You're not wrong, little sage. One day you must share your wisdom with less wise people. I'll teach you how to write out your ideas and stories. You will become a great and famous writer. One day, nearly everyone in Canada will have heard of your books, Isabelle."

"What is Canada?" we asked her. She got quiet.

Matthieu and I had now been married for seven years. My brother Lentug, a healer, had taught Matthieu many of our customs: when to collect medicinal plants at their greatest potency and how to use them to cure illnesses; how to read the weather; and how to know when the time had come for the indwelling spirit to surrender to the end of the body and begin the journey forward—into the starry fields far above the earth. We call the spirits' road *Skedegmujuawti,* the Milky Way.

In the late autumn, some weeks after Diane's ominous warning about the Europeans, my brother and Matthieu returned to the island after one of their long journeys away. They told us that they had heard rumblings among the French traders. "They say the English have a strategic plan, you see: they're attempting to take over key settlements as their boats sail along the Saint Lawrence River toward Quebec," explained Matthieu.

"Yes," Lentug said. "Just last week, a small group of locals heroically fought off some English soldiers at Rivière-Ouelle—not that far from us.

Cacouna Island is also on the way to Quebec. I foresee trouble for us."

My brother convinced my husband that we needed to shift the sacred glacial rock, our protector for generations, off the island. "Our new home lies over there." He pointed to the mainland. "I've spoken to a young farmer—Bernard Beaumont—who's just settled a nice piece of land and who says we're welcome to live next to him. I'll help you build a beautiful new home for Wasaweg, Matthieu, in Bernard's clearing in the wood that slopes down to the beach and the river. I have given him part of the payment already."

I disagreed with Lentug's counsel and, rare for me, raised my voice. "No! Why move? You should have consulted me, brother! Cacouna Island belongs to the Great Spirit—who lets us live on his land as guests," I said, adamant. "This buying and selling idea belongs to the foreigners. Forsake your claim. I refuse to leave our land."

My brother had that faraway stare that always misted over his eyes when he would prophesy. "Your descendants will flourish and multiply, Wasaweg. But our time here has ended. Any day the English will invade this sanctuary. They are inimical to the French—our allies. War looms over our holy island like brooding, dark clouds. Lightning jabs at the sky, soon to strike and shake the ground like a spear. Our people will scatter as ashes in wind. Our *only* hope is to dwell close to the sacred stone given to our people by the Long White Wave. The stone will be the bedrock of your new home, Wasaweg, and our kith and kin. *Gisawaug* must be moved to the site of this new home on the mainland."

A few weeks passed. The autumn light streamed down. Late one afternoon, Diane and I were relaxing after a long day's work. All day we had picked berries and gathered wild cherries and apples; our fingers were stained blue and scarlet. Winter loomed. We needed to gather and dry fruit for the cold, dark months ahead.

Out of the blue, Diane asked, "Wasaweg, do you think your brother will ever marry?"

"No. I don't, because as a healer, Lentug will serve the people—not his individual desires and feelings."

Diane got quiet and became thoughtful, even sad. I wondered if perhaps she and Lentug felt attracted to one another. Ever since Matthieu had found Diane unconscious on the beach and brought her home to live with us, I'd seen my brother sneak curious looks in her direction.

Emboldened, I asked, "Why do you ask? Do you have romantic feelings for Lentug?"

"Strangely, his presence reminds me of someone I loved long ago, but I consider that man my only soul mate. I can never love anyone as I love him."

I nodded. "Of course."

Diane didn't say anything for a few minutes. "I never talk about him, because he's so far away now. I don't know if I'll ever see him again. The last time I saw him, we were in the middle of a quarrel. An earthquake happened. He got trapped. I still don't know if he got out. I think of him all the time, you know, especially at night, when I'm not busy. I just hope that time is passing quicker for him than it is for me."

I must have looked hurt, because she hastened to assure me.

"It's not that I'm unhappy here, Wasaweg! If my beloved were with me, I'd never want to leave Cacouna Island. I'd have my whole family around me—" She stopped herself as if she were holding back from revealing something she didn't think I could hear. "This has been such an unbelievable, magical time living with your family. You've been so kind to me, like a sister … But I am sad now, because, you see, my time in New France is over. Matthieu told me about Lentug's plan to move the sacred stone and settle your family on the mainland. When you leave, I'll go back to my people."

"I understand." I reached out and took her hand.

"But tell me, how will Lentug lift the rock? He can't do it singlehandedly. Even if a hundred warriors were to lift it up and place it in a canoe, they couldn't get it across the water to the mainland; Gisawaug is too heavy."

"The sacred stone will be lifted and moved, Diane, by the power of thought alone."

"I don't understand."

"Our community will join together our thoughts. A group of people can, by holding hands tightly, form a human chain. So think how much strength will arise if we unite our collective minds! We'll merge our inner powers and create a great, superhuman force."

"I see," she said doubtfully—as if she did not see.

"Faith moves mountains, so why can our rock not be lifted? Don't you believe?"

Diane smiled. "In my own way, I do." A wistful look clouded her eyes. "I remember my mother told me she thought that those who pray help maintain some measure of peace in the world."

It was the first time Diane had ever mentioned her mother. I wondered if she had started missing her parents as well as her beloved and if that was also why she wanted to leave us. "Will you stay for the bonfire at least?" I asked. "The sacred stone will be moved tomorrow at midnight."

"I wouldn't miss it for the world." She smiled at me as she stood up and brushed the leaves from her dress.

I still remember her walking off toward her wigwam as twilight descended. I called out: "Thank you for all your help today!"

It was my way of appreciating the years she'd spent living as part of our family.

# FIVE: LE FLEUVE D'ARGENT (THE SILVER RIVER)

*Saint Jean Baptiste Day, twenty-first century*

Sarah checked her messages. "Hey, friend! Matt Landry here. Been a while! I met your house guest Deanna and neighbour Pierre the other day. I invited them to the Saint Jean Baptiste bonfire. Hope you all come over our way tonight. It would be so great to see you again." Pierre had pulled a muscle when he lifted a rock while landscaping (he forgot to bend his knees) and so opted out of going to the party. Deanna, Justin, and Sarah left the guesthouse for the First Nation Centre after supper, heading for the gravel road that led to the beach. The sun's slow descent toward the blue mountains on the distant North Shore coincided with the pale moon's rising above the South Shore's sloping hills.

    The gravel road down to the beach skirted the ruins of a farm. Sarah pointed to old foundation stones that poked through long grass and straggling weeds. "The farmhouse burned down a few years after A.Y. Jackson rented a room in it."

    "My mom told me," Deanna interjected, "that A.Y. Jackson visited Cacouna many times. He stayed in a different home each year."

    "Yes. They called him Père Raquettes, Father Snowshoes, because he went out on snowshoes with his easel and paints. The snowshoes allowed him to keep his balance on the snow and paint still-lifes." Sarah chuckled. "He and my great aunt's husband, Uncle Fred, could have been friends, we figure—Uncle Fred was an artist, too."

"That sketch that hangs in your kitchen—of an old woman stirring a pot on a woodstove—is that one of your uncle Fred's?" asked Justin.

"Yup. We sold the original oil painting last year to pay for the new water pump. This is just a print."

"F.W.H was your great uncle?" Deanna looked impressed. "Mum has one of his works in her office at the museum. He was a great Canadian artist, although not that well known."

"Of course I never met him," Sarah continued. "He died long before I was born. But I adore his paintings. The mountains on the North Shore were his inspiration."

"They're lovely," Deanna said. "I still like to believe they're blue." She smiled.

"The North Shore inspired other Canadian artists, too. Our family friend Paul Almond filmed *Journey* on the Saguenay River."

"We heard about him, didn't we, on CBC. How did you meet?"

"He asked my mom to help promote his books in the Alford Saga."

"I didn't know your mother worked as a book publicist."

"Sometimes." Sarah smiled. "We can go for months without guests when the snow piles up—past the windowsills mid-winter. So, in her free time, Mom works freelance and helps arrange authors' book launches. She felt honoured to work with Paul. He had phenomenal energy and was so generous with his time.

When most people would have been enjoying their retirement in their golden years, he, even in his eighties, crisscrossed Canada to speak with Canadians about our history. His homestead was on the Gaspé, where he and his wife Joan spent their summers. I was just a child when Paul died, but my mother told me he was a mentor to her and many people. Paul made everyone feel special."

Deanna linked her arm through Sarah's. They walked in silence for a few minutes, the gravel crunching under their feet.

"Deanna and I want to get across to Tadoussac next weekend and go whale watching on the Saguenay," Justin said after a few minutes.

"You'll love the ferry ride across the river. It skirts the reefs and usually you can see hundreds of seals sunbathing—if it's a sunny day, that is. Bring binoculars."

"You know—" Deanna interjected. "That seal in Wasaweg's wall-hanging seems to stare at you—from whatever angle you look at it."

"Ah, so you went into the barn. Did you notice…" Sarah began. Just then, the road veered toward a steep cliff. "Hey, guys, check it out! Belugas!"

Beyond the reefs, snow white whales were rising in and out of the river.

"The tide's high," she continued. "You'll see them play like this for hours. *Écoute!*" She put a finger to her lips. "Do you hear the seals howling?"

Deanna listened. She squinted. Black flecks dotted the nearest reef, less than a quarter of a kilometre offshore. The sunset began to streak rose, gold, and crimson across the sky.

They walked in silence. The light on the water shimmered and stretched before them—a vast, silver mirror reflecting the colour-suffused sky—soon to be swallowed up by total night. "We locals call it *le Fleuve d'Argent*," Sarah said. "The Silver River."

"It sounds much nicer in French," Deanna said.

"*Everything* sounds nicer in French," Justin added.

On the beach, they sidestepped a rusty chain and the top of an anchor that lay, half submerged, in sand. "So many shipwrecks ... The Saint Lawrence is beautiful, but she is dangerous," Sarah said.

"That's interesting. You're the second person to say that to me since I reached Cacouna," Deanna said.

Wild rose bushes, thick with magenta blooms, lay between the dirt road that wound along the shoreline and the pebble-strewn beach with its rust-coloured shale. The hedges continued for kilometres, sometimes growing so tall that the fragrance almost dripped down on the three walkers. They decided to rest by the water for a few minutes, so they plunked their knapsacks on Sarah's picnic blanket which she spread out above the high tide mark. Justin walked down to the river and tested the water temperature. He shivered. "Pretty cold. Wouldn't want to go swimming today."

Deanna left the others and scrambled up a rock that jutted out into the Saint Lawrence. She dipped her feet in the salt river. "Don't mind me," she yelled back.

"I'm just going to sit here for a few minutes and take in the view."

"Don't slip in! You'd freeze!" Justin yelled.

She wiggled her feet in the water and gazed at the clouds. They hovered above like people silently watching her. She loved the way they reached up—like feathers, or fingers yearning to clasp some unseen hand.

All day she'd had a restless feeling in the pit of her stomach. She closed her eyes, feeling the last remnants of sunlight return momentarily from behind the veil of clouds and warm the surface of her body.

Suddenly, a powerful undertow tugged at her legs and, in surreal slow motion, she witnessed her body being dragged out into the water by the inexorable grip of the ice cold current. She didn't resist. To flail against an undertow meant sure death. She felt numb, shocked, and, in the spinning, endlessly stretching moments that elapsed before she lost consciousness, she witnessed a thought flitting through her mind: *This is exactly what happened the moment Matthew vanished. In a split second, I felt frozen. I knew—he's gone and he won't return.*

When she came to, rough, brittle reef rock was scraping her belly; the pain brought her consciousness fully back. The current had carried her, and, inexplicably, had lifted her body up on the edge of the closest reef. She pulled herself up onto the rock and gasped for breath.

"Deanna," a deep voice bellowed.

Her heart thudded. She turned her head. In the misty twilight, a lone seal lumbered toward her. She thought if she turned on her side and lay completely still it might ignore her, but it edged closer to her, its flippers skimming over the rocks. She sat up. It bore the body of a seal, but, for a moment, she glimpsed her brother—soft black eyes, deep pools of sorrow and love and tears.

"I miss you all the time. I see you everywhere. I can't bear it." Her tears slipped out. She swallowed. "Matthew, if it's you, which seems impossible, tell me something only you would know."

The seal threw itself at her feet and spoke in Matthew's resonating baritone. "That thing that happened in the museum with the painting … You know, one minute I stood beside you, the next moment—you were gone, and so was I …"

"I knew I wasn't insane." She stared at him through her tears. "I didn't make it up. It's driven me half crazy sometimes, not knowing, not understanding what happened, why you …" She couldn't tell if they were using actual words or if they were now communicating telepathically. Sometimes his eyes would look like a seal's eyes and then the seal face would dissolve and she'd see Matthew's face and his deep black eyes. "Why aren't you human?" she cried. "Are you a ghost?"

"No, no! I still exist, Deanna. I had to reach you somehow, so I assumed this dream form—just to let you know my existence was not snuffed out even though I disappeared. Don't cry. I'll tell you what happened. When I looked at that painting, I remembered my other life, or, maybe, my other life remembered me. In that life, I sailed to New France, where I settled and married a beautiful Mi'gmaq woman. We had two gorgeous and loving children—a little girl, Isabelle, and a healthy baby boy—Matthis. I dreamed of you and Mum and Dad every night, but I'd forget those dreams in the morning, because I loved my life with Wasaweg on Cacouna Island."

"Wasaweg? The woman whose journal I'm reading? Oh my God, Matthew! How can you be both my brother Matthew *and* Matthieu Landry, the man Wasaweg married? I don't understand …Matthew, don't go … no, please … don't leave me again."

"You're having a nightmare, honey." Justin was stroking her head. The rock was icy cold beneath her body. She had fallen asleep by the river.

"I was talking to my brother, to Matthew! Why did you wake me up? Let me get back to my dream—maybe I'll see him again." She closed her eyes, but the dream was finished. The reunion with Matthew had been a mere mental fabrication, not a vision. Her clothing wasn't even wet—she couldn't possibly have swum out to the reef.

Sarah looked at her with tears in her eyes. "I'm so sorry about your loss. I know you're suffering. You miss your brother." She paused. "Deanna, you kept calling out 'Wasaweg.' I think it's time to put her diary away, hon. You're getting way too involved in her story."

Justin pulled Deanna up and hugged her close. He wiped away the tears that smeared her face. Her body was shaking with the cold. "Come on. Let's go to the Saint Jean Baptiste party. The bonfire will warm and cheer you up." He helped her back into her socks and shoes. Sarah rolled up the picnic blanket and stuffed it into her knapsack.

Deanna, still dazed, stared at her surroundings. She didn't say a word. They started walking briskly toward the First Nation Centre and the bonfire.

# SIX: TOUCH NOT THE PAINTING

*One year earlier, the Montreal Museum of Fine Arts*

The museum exhibition hall was filled with dappled light and shadows. Matthew heard the sound of voices in the next room. His sister tugged at his sleeve. "Get a move on, Matthew. We're late. Mum's already emceeing speeches in the other room." He moved to leave. On his way out, he stopped in front of a small painting of an old sailing ship. One man in the painting had greying hair. The other was a young man with handsome features, an aquiline nose, strong chin, dark hair, dark eyes. Both men wore old-fashioned European clothing. *My God that guy looks just like me. How weird.*

The younger man's arm rested on the ship's wheel. A blue flag fluttered in the stern; the French coat of arms—emblazoned on a white cross—rippled in the wind.

Matthew stepped closer to read the silver plaque at the base of the frame: 'Sieur Charles de Beaumont and Captain Matthieu Landry Set Forth for New France'.

He knew he shouldn't touch it—how often had Mum told them never to touch paintings in the museum—but Matthew reached out anyway. He gingerly ran his hand along the frame. Suddenly his body began to shake and quiver as if an electric current had shot through his arm. He couldn't let go of the picture frame! His ears started ringing, or was it the sound of the sea he heard? The crashing waves got louder. He felt a cool breeze touch his face and tasted salt from the spray of the waves as they struck the ship's wooden sides. Was he still looking at the painting or was he now *in* the painting? Realities blurred. Then, one deafening roar and the ground cracked below his feet. The museum walls had vanished. Deanna was gone. He was floundering in the water, flailing his arms and calling for help. He passed out.

\*\*\*

When he awoke, he stood alone on a rocky beach. The air was thick with the scent of seaweed. A wide river stretched before him. Purplish-blue mountains rose up on the distant shore through the mist. The light in the sky was different, cleaner, and clearer. Even the forest looked younger, greener somehow. His head ached and his heart pounded.

Half a dozen men raced toward him. Their long homespun robes billowed in the wind. The leader shouted in French: "Follow us! To the monastery! Your enemies are in pursuit and hunt you. You'll be safe with us."

Matthew caught up to the priests in no time. They raced through a field adjacent to the beach. A newly carved wooden cross marked a grave. Wild bluebells and lilies of the valley piled up in a fragrant heap on a mound of earth. He stopped and sucked in his breath sharply. The inscription on the cross read: *Thierry Lefevre. Died at Kakona, New France, on June 15, 1683, Anno Domini.* A young priest stopped. He whispered to Matthew: "Happened last week. Thierry's heart gave out." He crossed himself.

A second priest yelled back at them: "Don't lag behind. Keep running! Charles de Beaumont and his men are hot on our heels. They swam to shore last night. Beaumont swears this man's a traitor and caused the ship to crash. It's utter nonsense. Anyone who saw the storm come up knows that it was Nature that wreaked havoc on the river. But anyway, the only safe place for him right now is our monastery."

The first priest, panting as he raced beside Matthew, said: "I heard you're on Beaumont's 'wanted' list. He's the most powerful businessman in New France. What in Heaven's name did you do, Matthieu Landry, to anger him and get a bounty placed on your head?!"

*Matthieu Landry? That young sea captain in the painting? Bounty on my head ... in 1683? How was that even possible?* His teeth had begun chattering and he felt the earth swim beneath his feet as he tried to keep up with the men who were trying to help him. He looked down to make sure he wouldn't trip on all the gravestones and crosses that covered the field. He noticed his pants and shirt were tattered and soaked. He glanced over at the river and saw that the high tide had littered the beach with broken planks of wood. Had he survived some surreal shipwreck or was he experiencing a total nervous breakdown?

He hadn't been himself lately. No, not since Deanna found the adoption papers two days ago in their father's study. They had been arguing about it at the museum. He told her he intended to ask his parents about it and demand why they kept it secret for almost twenty years, but she wanted him to first look into it on his own and had offered her help. "Easy for you to say," he had said to her. "You're not the one who just found out that you were adopted. At least now I know why I never fit in …"

He heard himself mindlessly repeating the date carved over the grave: "Kakona, 1683." His legs buckled. Rough, calloused hands picked him up—a burly young man slung him over his back.

They laid him on a narrow bed in a dimly lit monastic cell. An oil lamp swung from the ceiling. Someone stripped off his cold, wet clothes. "He's delirious," an old man's voice said. "Wrap him in warm blankets and put a heated stone by his feet. Let's hope he makes it through the night."

***

Matthew glanced around the tiny room. Daylight streamed through the window. A robin sidestepped along the windowsill and peeked in.

He stood up and pushed his legs out of bed. They felt shaky, as if he had just gotten off a boat after a long journey. Was he in a hospital? Had he drunk too much wine? Then he sank back onto the lumpy straw mattress and cupped his face in his hands. He remembered the night before. He remembered the jolt of power that had wracked his body when he touched the painting's frame. His thoughts flew first to his sister. How horrible for Deanna to witness. One moment he had been standing next to her, and then he vanished.

*She must be beside herself now. What would she tell our parents?* She'd have to concoct some story because the truth was too mind-blowing.

He knew he'd be on a list of missing persons. They'd check all the flights leaving Trudeau Airport. He had no way to let his family know he was alive. Then he recollected the date on the small wooden cross in the field by the river. The physical shock that had catapulted him through time had been quite horrible, but now the mental shock was even worse. 1683. The year was 1683 and he was a French sea captain with a bounty on his head. He knew he had traveled back in time to when French settlers were still establishing themselves on the shores of what would be later called Canada. Could this be Quebec centuries ago—when it was part of New France? Was he really Matthieu Landry—a French explorer hunted down by the most powerful businessman in New France? In the twenty-first century, he was on a "list of missing persons." In 1683, he was on a "wanted list."

The door creaked open. A young boy carried a tray with a jug of hot water and a bowl of hot food.

"Père Michel said to check on you. Do you need anything else?"

Matthew shook his head. He nibbled on a piece of bread and gratefully sank back onto the narrow bed. Perhaps, if he could sleep, he'd reawaken in his familiar world. Deanna would be still at his side, the museum walls wouldn't have melted away, and this strange dream would fade.

\*\*\*

A few hours later, the boy returned to his room.

"Père Michel thought you'd enjoy this book." He placed a thick journal by Father Chrétien Le Clercq on a side table.

After the boy left, Matthew began to read. He was glad his parents had encouraged him to go to a French CEGEP and become fluent in French. Nonetheless, the priest used a few antiquated, obsolete French expressions. He wished he had a dictionary.

"The Mi'gmaq believe that when they die, they rise up to the stars; afterwards, they enter beautiful green meadows with fair trees, flowers, and rare fruit …" He flipped to another section of the book. "In their *wigwams*, many healers possess manuscripts, full of pictures etched into pieces of bark or stone, which they read over sick persons. They say they can express any idea by these signs, just as Europeans do with their writings."

At supper, he asked Père Michel about the book. The priest explained how it had fallen into his hands. "Eight years ago, Father Chrétien Le Clercq, under Governor Frontenac's orders, sailed from France and landed at Percé in Gaspésie. Perhaps you've heard of Father Le Clercq? He has spent years living with the Mi'gmaq—from Percé to Miramichi. Well, about four years ago, on a journey to Quebec, he stopped in at our monastery. Le Clercq is from the Recollet Order in France, and it was heartwarming for me to spend time with such a learned man of God. I invited him to remain with us for a fortnight as he was very tired from his journey. He and I spent many a night by the fire reading scripture together, praying, and talking about our hopes for the people who are settling this land. We talked at length about the Mi'gmaq who were here long before the settlers arrived. He opened my eyes to their culture and ways. He has even begun learning their language." The old man sipped his water. "The Mi'gmaq, Le Clercq explained to me, use mnemonic storytelling—utilizing drawings to trigger the memory of a story. This is a technique vital to older cultures throughout the world. They often communicate similar symbols. I suppose that's not surprising," the priest mused. "Pictures transcend language: they're a far deeper and more effective way of transmitting wisdom than ordinary words."

"You know so much about the indigenous people, Père Michel. How long have you been here in New France?" The words 'New France' sounded strange to Matthew as soon as he had spoken them; nevertheless, he was, despite his shock and misgivings about being jolted out of the twenty-first century, beginning to be increasingly curious about this wild and unknown land to which he had time travelled.

"My ancestors, fishermen, sailed from the Basque area and settled in Acadia. My grandfather started a family on the coast. One year, the fishing season fell short and the winter that followed was especially brutal. Both of my parents died of scurvy. Grandpapa was too poor to provide for us, his grandchildren, you see, and so when a group of missionaries promised to take care of me and my brother, he allowed the Jesuit priests to adopt us. I owe my life to them, but I don't see eye to eye with everything they teach. Some overzealous missionaries refer to the indigenous people as savages. All too few Christians recognize them—the original dwellers of this land. They are the First Peoples—many peoples, many nations, living upon one land. They welcomed the French in the beginning. It is we Europeans who acted savagely toward them, and, the worst of it, if you ask me, is that we have done so in the name of our Lord who is all love."

A long and comfortable silence followed. Matthew stretched his feet out toward the fireplace. He was starting to feel at home in this place. It was so quiet. No cell phones beeping text messages, no blaring TV, no harsh neon lights or hidden cameras on street corners. Everything looked rugged, yet, paradoxically, everything seemed softer and more refined.

"One thing troubles me, Père Michel. You mentioned earlier at dinner about me going over to Kakoua-Nak Island and that the Mi'gmaq would take me in. I don't understand."

The priest's face grew somber. "I'm so sorry to have to ask you to leave our monastery, but while you were sleeping, I heard distressing news—Sieur Charles de Beaumont's men hover close by. They are in the village. They *will* hunt you down, Matthieu. Alas, your presence among us may well provoke an attack on my brethren. You must slip out of our monastery and canoe to Kakoua-Nak Island before dawn breaks."

"I'll find food and shelter on the island?"

"Yes. The Mi'gmaq have survived on the island as long as I've known. It's not far from here—just a short canoe ride away. If you're respectful of their ways, they'll befriend you and offer refuge."

## SEVEN: "THE LETTER KILLS, BUT THE SPIRIT GIVES LIFE"

It was around ten at night that the door creaked opened yet again. Matthew jumped up. It was a girl of about sixteen and she had a small cat in her arms. "Je m'excuse," (I'm sorry), she said. Both she and the animal had the same wide-eyed and frightened look. *The innocent are not allowed to live innocently,* he suddenly thought.

"What's wrong? Are you hurt?" He saw a red welt across her cheekbone. Whoever had struck her had narrowly missed her eye.

"Mother Superior …" she began and burst out sobbing.

"She struck you?!"

"Yes, with a stick, but that's not why I'm crying, Monsieur Landry. She strikes me daily. But you know, sir, she told me she will get rid of my cat tomorrow morning. I'm worried she will throw little Bellevue into the pond and drown her." The girl's thin body was wracked with grief. "Mother Superior said: 'Cats and dogs have no place in the kingdom of heaven.' And she said that because it's a black cat, it is the devil's spawn—it steals my attention away from devotion to the Lord. She warned me if I continue to let Bellevue sleep in my room, I, too, will be thrown out of the convent."

Matthew recalled that he'd seen a building just left of the monastery and had wondered who lived there. Now he knew. "Oh! So you live in the convent next door," he said.

"Yes. In the Sacred Shelter of the Sisters of Saint Augustine. I'm sorry for my tears. Please excuse me."

"It's understandable. What's your name?"

"I'm Émilie. I'm a novice," the girl continued. "I'll take my vows next year, when I am seventeen."

*So young,* Matthew thought. *But perhaps taking shelter in a convent had been her best option. Many girls as young as sixteen were married off to men three or four times their age in the early days of New France.*

As if she'd read his thoughts, she said, "My father arranged for me to marry a settler in the New World. He stuffed me onto a ship where I had to spend weeks crammed in with hundreds of other young girls."

"*Les filles du Roi,*" he said. (The king's daughters.)

"Yes, Papa said it would be a great honour. We received fifty livres because I was to marry a soldier. I was even given a 'hope chest' full of clothing and a sewing kit."

Matthew couldn't believe it. He'd read about this in Canadian history text books in high school. Hundreds of young French women immigrated to New France as wards of King Louis XIV to increase the nation's population. Matthew had read that the mission ended in 1673, but, obviously, many parents had continued to send their daughters to the new country. The plan to populate New France had succeeded at the cost of hundreds of young women forced to leave everyone they knew and loved in France. He'd never really thought twice about it when he read that chapter of Canada's history. Never wondered how each girl reacted when they were sent away from their families and homeland and had to cross the ocean to marry a stranger.

"You know, sir," Émilie continued, "I have loved Jesus Christ my whole life. My mother and I used to pray together every night before bed. I couldn't believe I had to marry that old man to whom they presented me at the altar. My father had been promised that I would marry a soldier just a few years older than me. So I cried out to the Lord, 'Save me! Let me be one of Jesus Christ's brides instead!' The priest who presided over the ceremony took pity."

"Père Michel?" Matthew guessed.

She nodded. "He is a *real* father. He shows compassion. He stopped the ceremony and said, 'If she's unwilling to marry this man, let her become a nun in the Sisters of Saint Augustine.' He sent me to the convent next door. But the Mother Superior is worse than an abusive husband. She discovered me feeding little Bellevue some of my leftover dinner," she kissed the cat in her arms, "and came to know I let my cat sleep in my cell, and she beat me with her stick! She told me she would order one of the boys to drown my cat tomorrow if I don't get rid of her myself."

"Oh my poor girl," Matthew said.

"Please, will you take Bellevue with you when you leave the monastery? My friend, Eugene, who brought you food earlier, told me you are leaving for Kakoua-Nak Island by dawn tomorrow. I know she's a good cat. She purrs in my lap when I recite my prayers. I don't understand why Mother Superior believes Bellevue distracts me from devotion to Lord Jesus. God is love. He lives in my heart. I have no parents here, not one of my brothers or sisters. I am all alone. Why would He not want me to feel comfort? Why would He not allow me to offer compassion to a little creature that he has made?"

"Yes, you are right. Never doubt your perception," Matthew said. "I, too, believe in the God of Love. Didn't Saint Paul say, 'The letter kills, but the Spirit gives life…'? *Christ* is infinite love and wisdom, but not all those who believe they have chosen the high road actually minister his love; rather, many judge others and lord over them even in Christ's name. It is an utter misuse of God's power and love. All you can do, Émilie, is vow to never become like them. Don't hate them, but stay out of their way; instead, devote your energy to that which gives you strength."

"So you will take my cat?" She gave a broad smile.

"Of course. Bellevue will come with me."

# EIGHT: KAKOUA-NAK ISLAND

*Kakoua-Nak Island, seventeenth century*

The little cat curled up at his feet, purring peacefully, but Matthew tossed, sleepless, in his bed. At first the river's waves crashed loudly against the rocks; later, a hushed silence fell over the night. The tide had gone way out. He smelled seaweed through the open window. A pale crescent moon rose in the sky and northern lights flashed: brilliant, pulsating sheets of white, glacial green, and pink. Eventually, the colours faded into darkness. Soon the sun would rise. It was time to leave the priests. He sat up in bed, stroked Bellevue under her chin, and got dressed in the warm clothes that Père Michel had given him. In the candlelight, he glimpsed his own reflection in the water basin as he washed his face. He looked like a French voyageur. He slipped Chrétien Le Clercq's journal into a large rucksack; the priest had said he could keep the book, as well as some extra clothes that had been provided to him. Last, he gently placed the cat into the bag, where it nestled in among the clothing. He left the top a little bit open so there would be enough air for her. He was worried she would meow and waken the priests as he crept by their cells, but she seemed to know that Matthew was her caretaker now and had saved her from a miserable fate. He, too, was ready for whatever lay ahead.

    Matthew knelt in the canoe, his rucksack ahead of him on the ribbed floor. The wind ruffled his hair and he felt strangely elated. His paddle cut swift, clean strokes in the still water. How effortless it was to steer a canoe, even though this was his first time canoeing. Perhaps he really had been Matthieu Landry in another life.

    As he paddled across to the island, he felt sorry to have left the priests, for they had been kind to him in his brief stay, but he couldn't shake off his awareness of how missionaries had mistreated indigenous people. He'd read in the six-thousand-page Truth and Reconciliation Commission report after it went public. He remembered watching a YouTube video of Canada's Prime Minister, tears in his eyes, greeting the First Nations in their own languages and apologizing to them on behalf of the Canadian government. The Prime Minister was to be commended for beginning to make amends for the atrocious injustices done to the first people of Canada. Their lands had been taken away and children separated from their parents—sent to residential schools to be "educated"—forced to forget their first tongue and the ways of their ancestors. Countless had died and were buried in unmarked graves. Indigenous women, who still went missing, were assaulted or murdered by people who had lost all respect for women's bodies and souls. He remembered one politician saying the women had gone missing because they had been unemployed. Unbelievable. Thank God that politician had resigned in shame.

    After some time, his paddle scraped rocks. He jumped into the icy water and waded to the beach, dragging the canoe ashore and wedging it between two trees far enough from the water that high tide wouldn't drag it away. He had no idea how long he would be on Cacouna Island.

He peeked into his bag and saw the small cat still sleeping on top of the extra clothes he had packed. "Here you go little kitty," he said as he gently lifted her out. "Be free. You're welcome to follow me if you want. I'll care for you best I can." He was amazed to see that she pranced behind him as he walked on the forest path.

"You're a dead man," a gravelly voice announced from behind a tree. In seconds, a skinny, haggard man jumped in front of him. Bellevue, of course, leaped into the bushes, ducking for cover. The man reeked of alcohol and manure. He pinned Matthew's wrists together in front and tied them with thick cord. The man tugged the knot so that the rope cut into his skin.

"Who are you?"

"Gérald Bouchard," the man grunted.

"What do you want?"

"My boy at the monastery tipped me off that you're on the run. I decided to leave last night so I could greet you." He smirked.

"Why? What's in it for you? What do you have against me?"

"I'm a poor farmer. My starving family needs the bounty Sieur Beaumont placed on your head."

"How much am I worth?" He was curious.

"Ten *deniers,* two beaver pelts, and a sack of cornmeal."

"So what will you do with me?"

"I heard about the abandoned Mi'gmaq well on the island. Nobody will find your body if I toss it into the pit in the middle of the forest. Now, no more talking! I'm a man of action, not words!" He yanked Matthew along by the rope, and charged off into the woods.

After trekking for less than an hour, they reached a stream. Gérald's gaunt face was dripping with sweat. He stooped down to drink fresh water. A whistling sound, followed by a thud, made both men turn their heads swiftly. A second arrow pierced some bushes and whizzed by; it lodged in the rope that bound Matthew's hands together and shredded the cord. The marksman was expert: he hadn't wanted to kill him, but rather to free him. The sudden release propelled Matthew to his knees. He lifted his head and looked into the dark brown eyes of a man about his age. Gérald, terrified, ran off into the woods.

The young man wore leather leggings and moccasins. A quiver full of arrows hung on his back. His black hair fell past his shoulders.

Before Matthew could say anything, from deep within the forest the enchanting melody of a flute sounded out. It was so beautiful he forgot everything for a moment. When he returned to his senses, he asked. "What is that?"

"It is the *Mi'gmwesu'g*. Beautiful and strong, the flute players save humans who are lost in the woods. It is a good omen. It means you have a high destiny. You were meant to be found by me today."

"*Merci. Vous m'avez sauvé la vie.* You saved my life," Matthew said.

The man helped him to his feet and said, "You can thank the *Mi'gmwesu'g* and my sister, Wasaweg. She sent me to find you."

"Who? I don't know anyone on this island. It's impossible. I've never visited before."

"Wasaweg had a vision of you last night. We've been waiting for you. I thought I'd come out and meet you."

"Who are you?"

"Lentug. I'm *puowin*—spiritual leader and healer in our clan. I am also *sagamaw,* or ruler."

"Your clan? Who are they?"

"We are Mi'gmaq. Long ago, my ancestors travelled here along the South Shore of the lower Saint Lawrence. We share the right of way on the river with the Wolastoqiyik and the Abenaki. Some of our people stopped here and fished and hunted in the summer season. Others chose to settle in this region. Many Mi'gmaq also live further east, around *Gespe'gewa'gi*– what the Europeans now call the Gaspé Peninsula—and beyond. My *mala*, home, lies close to the forest spring— the village well. First, we must walk through these woods awhile more."

"That man told me the well was abandoned."

"A mere rumour." Lentug dismissed his words with a flick of his hand. "The foreigners don't know a thing about our ways and life. They speak lies and say we are a doomed and conquered people. But we've been living on this island for generations already. We thrive, and you know what?—we'll survive." He smiled.

Just then, they heard a meow. They both turned their heads. The cat emerged from the bushes and rubbed against Matthew's ankles.

"Seems like you brought a friend," Lentug said. "Or perhaps the friend has followed you. Most welcome, both of you."

Lentug and Matthew walked, in silence, along a path that was all but invisible to the naked eye. As they walked, it all came back to him, everything he had studied in textbooks in high school. Before contact with the Europeans, the Mi'gmaq had numbered in the tens of thousands. The explorers, missionaries, and European settlers (Dutch, French, and English) had brought multiple diseases: smallpox, dysentery, and alcoholism. First the French had usurped the First Nations' lands. And then the English had done the same. What a horrible legacy the Europeans had left behind in their wake!

They were on the far side of the island, Lengtug explained, where a hidden trail would take them up to the top of the cliff to another trail leading over the rocky hilltop to Lentug's village. The back way was long and very strenuous, and they would have to double back along the second path, but this was worth it to avoid any more of Beaumont's men who might be lurking if news had spread that the sea captain had left the Jesuit monastery.
At long last they reached a wild, rocky beach looking out toward the distant north shore of the great river. The tide was out and pools of dark water gleamed in the sunlight. Matthew squinted and put his hand above his eyes to see better. He glimpsed mountains far away on the other side of the river. Along the rocks and shingle and patches of sand, huge boulders rested—

giants from another age. One of them was as tall as a two-storey house. The rocks were pale green as if, by being constantly draped in seaweed for millennia, the algae had dipped them in green dye. Their edges were rounded; they looked like stone carvings. Matthew thought of the Henri Moore exhibit at the museum. His mother loved Moore's works. But those pieces, however majestic and awe-inspiring, would pale if placed next to these sea-hewn sculptures. They were the real thing. No artifice. No human touch. Raw creation—the outcome of Nature's massive, creative force.

He gasped at what he saw next—a ring of standing stones further out in the water, with but a few metres between them. Matthew wasn't religious in a traditional sense, but it was clear to him that some higher power had placed the giant stones there. They were six metres high, seven metres wide. They could not have been moved by man, yet, clear as day, they had been arranged in a ring: silent, unmoved sentinels—not insentient stone—pillars of the Supreme Being. As if he had read his mind, Lentug said, "Thousands of moons ago, the Great River, *Mijioqon,* and the distant sea lay deep in frozen slumber. When the White Plains stirred awake and began to melt and move, these rocks broke away. They were carried from afar by the Great Moving Ice. It carried them to this sacred site." He climbed up one of the boulders and sat crossed-legged on the glacial rock—as if drawing on Earth's ancient power. "The Europeans," he continued, "spread false tales that we travelled here from another country and continent. They say we walked over *umgumi,* the ice. But I tell you, friend, we were always here: we are the First People of this land. The English and the French will never acknowledge it." Lentug clambered down from the rock. "Now we will climb." He pointed to a rocky cliff sparsely decorated by a few straggling spruce trees.

"Up that?" Matthew sucked in his breath, shocked.

"I will be right behind you. Look only at the path just ahead. Place your soles firmly on the rocks and dig your toes into the earth. The path winds up along the cliff's crevices. Don't look at what lies below. Don't gaze up at the sky. Don't turn your head to either side. Keep your eyes fixed on the narrow path. Foot, step, foot, step. Keep that beat and concentrate. All will be well."

When they finally hauled themselves over the top of the cliff, Lentug patted him on the back and said, "Good, my friend. You have passed the first test. Stay with us a while. Learn the Mi'gmaq ways. Share our water, eat our food, sing and celebrate with us. Bathe in the healing waters of *Mijioqon*—the great river." Lentug pointed at the shoreline of the Saint Lawrence River lying far below. The standing stones seemed to float on the silvery water, for the tide had begun to come in while they climbed the cliff.

"You call me 'friend.' Even though I'm a stranger?"

Lentug laughed. "We're all strangers in the world. Human beings are nomads—here only for a short visit. So why should we not be friends to one another? All of us depend on Mother Earth for existence. Every two-legged being, four-legged animal, winged or finned creature comes from the One, the Great Spirit. And now, friend, we are nearing my village."

They set off toward the healer's home. The trail remained almost invisible, but Lentug always knew where to tread. Bellevue seemed tired and Matthew picked her up and nestled her inside his jacket. She slept, purring peacefully.

Well-camouflaged wigwams rose up ahead of them in a clearing next to a stream. The frames of the lodges had been built out of stripped spruce saplings and covered with bands of bent hardwood, to which were fastened long panels of birch bark that formed a thatched roof. Smoke arose from a small fire set in a ring of stones inside the circle of wigwams. A young woman was playing with a small boy outside one of the wigwams. When she saw Lentug and his companion emerge from the woods, she called out, "Welcome!" She turned to Lentug, "My dream bodes well, brother," and smiled.

"Our friend has had a difficult time. I told him he could stay with us for the summer, longer if he likes."

"I'm Wasaweg," she introduced herself shyly. "Most of the villagers are away. The older children wanted to swim in the cold river, for the sun beats too brightly this afternoon. You must be thirsty. Drink." She offered him water. Grateful, he sat down on a log and sipped the drink. The cat stirred inside his jacket and he took Bellevue out and placed her in his lap. She started purring as he and Wasaweg stroked her sleek black fur.

"She seems right at home," said Lentug. "She looks a bit thin and hungry though."

While Lentug went to get some food for the cat, Matthew looked around. The peace was palpable. Soft green spruce branches swayed in a gentle summer breeze. Other than birds, the forest was totally silent and calm. To his surprise, Wasaweg sank onto the ground and sat by his knees.

"I've dreamed of you so many times," she said softly and smiled. "I'm glad you're here. This will be your home now."

He started to tell her she was mistaken, but when he looked into her eyes, his words got lost. All memory of the past and future disappeared into her warm dark eyes. He was with the Mi'gmaq now. He wanted to remain with Wasaweg forever.

# NINE: WASAWEG AND MATTHIEU

*Eleven months later*
*May 1684, New France*

Wasaweg and Matthieu walked hand in hand along the beach on the mainland at sunset, heading toward their canoe to go back to their home on the island. It had been a warm day and they were carrying their moccasins. They could see the North Shore in the distance, and Kakoua-Nak Island closer by. The tide was still coming in over the rocks and sand. Between the few stretches of sand, rough pebbles bruised their bare feet. Wild roses grew on bushes that stretched far along the river. The air was filled with the scent of the rose-blooms, and of seaweed. Snow white whales and small porpoises rose to the surface and dove back into the waters, again and again, their dance a magic of pure freedom. The reefs were dotted with seals, mere points in the distance; every so often some would move or disappear.

Soft, billowing clouds changed hue: grey, gold, blue, and pink; the wild grasses and trees were silhouetted in the twilight.

Wasaweg sat down on a boulder covered in seaweed and dangled her feet in the salty water, less chilly than usual on this warm day. Matthieu joined her and put his arms around her.

"Look, Wasaweg! *Gisigua'gu!* (An old seal!) See? Over there—on the rock."

"You speak our language well," she said. "I wish I could speak French as easily; it would help me feel more at home when we move to France."

"I've been thinking, Wasaweg. Why leave? In Europe, diseases will endanger you and our soon-to-be-born child; you'll have to acclimatize to a totally new country. You'll miss your family and your people's ways. You know, most native people who depart for France from this land don't survive."

"I had only thought you might grow homesick, Matthieu. If you're content living with my family, let's raise our children here, in the atmosphere of freedom. Whatever makes you happy, my love."

"I heard good news today. Charles de Beaumont has left the region and moved upriver, to the big settlement at Quebec. So the threat that's been looming over my head is gone. We're free to live anywhere now, even on the mainland. But, you know, I'd like to live out my days on Kakoua-Nak Island—with you and your kin."

"It sounds good." She smiled. "My family is your family now."

He stroked her long black hair, which the wind had made unkempt, and gazed at her. "You're so beautiful. I half imagine you're a dream. Like a mermaid, you may vanish any time now in the water." He plucked a piece of seaweed off the rock. "All I'd be left with of this moment would be a strand of seaweed and doubt you ever existed. When a person's gone, what use are memories and pictures when they drew their meaning from the person's actual presence?"

"Bodies, mental images, and feelings, they'll all dissolve in time," she said. "But true love never fades. It's like the Sun to the Moon of life's moods. Our oneness with each other, Matthieu Landry, is unchanging. You'll not forget this moment; if you do, I promise, I'll reach you in every lifetime to remind you of me and what we share!" She slid off the rock into the water and gazed up. "The water's lovely, darling. Jump in!"

# TEN: THE SAINT JEAN BAPTISTE WEEKEND

*Twenty-first century Cacouna, Quebec, Canada*

*Did I actually see a fantastical, talking seal or am I flipping out?* Deanna wondered as they continued walking quickly along the beach toward the First Nation Centre and the bonfire. While Sarah and Justin were talking about everyday matters, Deanna thought about the conversation she had had with her brother in her dream. *Maybe Matthew simply tried to use a dream to communicate to me that he's still alive.*

By the time they reached the party on the beach, Deanna's mood had perked up; she felt that inexplicable sense of lightheartedness that hope brings when it finally returns.

The flames roared. Sparks crackled and vanished in the darkening evening sky. Sarah steered her guests over to a silver-haired elderly woman. The woman was sitting in a pine deck chair a couple of metres from the fire. A navy blue wool shawl covered her shoulders. "Ann Godridge, I'd like you to meet Justin Roy and Deanna Aynsworth."

They shook hands politely. After making small talk about the great weather, Justin veered off to a side table to get some snacks. Deanna lingered near the fire.

"Pull up a chair."

"Thank you. Lovely to meet you, Mrs. Godridge."

"Call me Ann." The woman's blue eyes twinkled.

"Have you lived in Cacouna your whole life?"

"I've been visiting Cacouna for eight decades. My grandparents started visiting the area in the early part of the twentieth century, my parents met here one summer, and they first brought me here when I was six weeks old, so Cacouna's in my blood! But our cottage isn't winterized, you know, so we only stay down for part of the year. During the winter, I live in Montreal. At the first sign of warmer weather, I take the train to Rivière-du-Loup. I spend as many months as I can at our summerhouse—until the first frost."

"You're so lucky! The Bas-Saint-Laurent region is gorgeous."

"First time visiting?"

Deanna smiled. "Yes. We took the bus down a couple of weeks ago."

"When I was a child, the train was pretty much the only way to get here. Even though we are Montrealers, our family always considered Cacouna to be our real home. Mother and Father were married in the Anglican church at Rivière-du-Loup. I was baptized in St. James Church over in the village. My brothers and sisters and I spent so many happy summers here. But now, you see, I'm the last of my generation to visit Cacouna. All the close friends and relatives who used to come here with me have passed on—to the other side." A wistful look clouded the old woman's eyes.

Ann reminded Deanna of Grandmother Aynsworth, who had died five years before. People like them belonged to a generation mostly long gone. They possessed treasure-troves of experience and wisdom, often hidden. "Tell me about the good old days."

The old woman sat up in her chair. "Before the Great Depression, people flocked to Cacouna in the hundreds, even thousands. They came from New York, Toronto, or Montreal—some even from England."

"So it was a trendy place to visit?"

"Damn right. Even Canada's first Prime Minister had a summerhouse over in Rivière-du-Loup. I forget who, but someone once said, 'the air in the Lower Saint Lawrence is like champagne.' Grandmother had TB, and Cacouna cured her. The whole region was famous for its healing, restorative properties. Savvy businessmen built resorts, racecourses, and the golf course. But after the Great Depression of 1929, many of those thousands of people who used to summer in Cacouna couldn't afford the luxurious lifestyle anymore.

"The other day, I saw a dear photo of the four Allan children sitting on the steps of Montrose—the mansion built for Sir Montagu Allan of the Allan Line shipping company. Poor Sir Montagu and his wife both outlived their children. Wealth is no guarantee of happiness. But you know that, don't you, my dear." She reached out and took Deanna's hand and gave an affectionate squeeze. Her elegant fingers were cold, worn with age, and bore a simple gold wedding band.

Deanna wondered if word about her own family's tragedy had reached the village or if Ann simply had good intuition. "Has Cacouna changed a lot over the decades?"

"Oh, yes! Now they dump millions of tons of waste into the Saint Lawrence River every year, two thirds of that untreated. But back then the beach was completely unspoiled and the river was pretty pure and unpolluted. Daily we swam until sundown and sailed out to the reefs. I can still remember, we used to watch hundreds of belugas swimming and frolicking as far as the eye could see. My husband was incensed when they built that port over on Gros-Cacouna, I remember." She twirled the wedding ring on her finger with a pensive smile. "He was upset that they blasted away part of the island to make it – totally spoiled the natural beauty. We both felt it would bring more noise and pollution. Nowadays there are concerns that underwater sounds could be harming the whales too, from ships or any kind of blasting."

"I read a study that we're down to nine hundred belugas in the Saint Lawrence area, whereas at the end of the nineteenth century, ten thousand were thriving in the river."

"Yes, they've become endangered. At one point they were killed deliberately; now it's other hazards. Beluga carcasses sometimes wash up on the river's shore. It's so sad. They get poisoned by all the chemical pollutants that humans use."

"What could be done to reverse all that?"

"Protect the river," Ann said. "I can see that you perceive its sacredness."

"Yes," said Deanna. "I just love it. I get lost listening to the sound of the waves and gazing at the

North Shore ..." She was quiet. The two shared a few moments of silent understanding.

"Oh now I've made you pensive by talking about the plight of the whales. I didn't mean to create a somber mood, especially on the Saint Jean Baptiste festival! Listen, Deanna, you should get out and about more. Go and see some of the marvelous places around here."

"I guess I *could*. Sarah keeps encouraging me to see the sights. And I do enjoy walking in nature."

"Then the island is the place for you! Gros-Cacouna marsh has an ornithological site. Have you heard about it?"

Deanna shook her head.

"It's a bird sanctuary with gorgeous trails. And if you do get over to Cacouna Island, visit the caves, too. I know they're technically off limits, but I wouldn't let an opportunity like that slip by, not if I were your age. No indeed." She winked at her.

"My boyfriend," Deanna pointed at Justin, who stood talking to someone on the other side of the bonfire, "is working over at the dig this summer. They've begun excavating the old Mi'gmaq settlement site—they've found some artifacts from the 1600s. Justin's fascinated with First Nations history. Told me he's been like that since he was a kid. But now that he's working on the site, he's frustrated. His supervisor won't let them look for the caves. Justin knows they are likely just a couple of kilometres away from the dig, and it's driving him crazy. You see, the moment he heard about the Cacouna Island cave drawings, he knew he wanted to examine them firsthand."

"A true scholar," Ann said, nodding. "If he gets permission to explore the caves, please tell him I'm interested and he should come and visit me and let me know all about them. You see, I'm the person who discovered Wasaweg's diary in my attic. I have no idea how it ended up there, but when I was a little girl I used to sit in the attic and read it. I've read it a dozen times over the years. I always believed that one day they would discover those caves on the island. And I still hope," she gave Deanna a pointed stare, "that someone will find out what happened to Matthieu Landry, find out who he really was and why he went missing."

Deanna's eyes widened; then she smiled. "I'll pass on your message to Justin for sure. Actually, we'd both love to visit you. I've enjoyed this talk so much! Thank you." She stood up and kissed Ann on both cheeks.

"Wonderful. I live just past the Cliff Cottages. Did I mention that before? Drop by around tea time any day. I'll serve you tea and cake on my porch. It overlooks those beautiful mountains on the other side of the river."

A tanker appeared in the distance. The sky was now purplish to navy blue streaked with the final remnants of the rose-gold sunset—soon to ebb into deep darkness. As Deanna walked away, she wondered about the cryptic words Ann had spoken. *Find out what happened to Matthieu Landry; find out who he really was and why he went missing.* And she heard the old woman singing a hymn quietly to herself:

"All things bright and beautiful,

All creatures great and small,
All things wise and wonderful,
The Lord God made them all.
The purple-headed mountain,
The river running by,
The sunset and the morning,
That brightens up the sky …"

Deanna walked around the bonfire to rejoin Justin and Sarah. Justin was deep in conversation with a tall man. "Sarah's writing a novel set in Cacouna; her neighbour, Pierre Desjardins, is building a website about Cacouna's history; and I'm working at the dig." He became aware of Deanna's presence. "Oh good! I wanted to introduce you to each other! My girlfriend—Deanna Aynsworth. Deanna—meet Émile Beaulieu. He's the nephew of the previous owners of Cacouna Island."

"Pleasure to meet you," she said, shaking his hand. "I didn't know the island had been owned privately. Who lives on it now?"

"A dozen private cottages lie on the north-eastern side of the island. The western end is occupied by the port of Gros-Cacouna – a deep-water port."

"And your relatives once owned the whole thing?" Her eyes glinted with excitement. "Awesome! You must know so much about its history."

"Yes." Émile smiled modestly. "It was even called 'Beaulieu Island' for some years. Probably that's because one uncle farmed the land there until 1977, and his dad and granddad had also spent their lives on the island. In 1962, my other uncle sold the western part."

"Who bought it?" Justin asked.

"It was purchased for construction of the port. Many people were not in favour of the seaport, although some would argue that it *has* been a plus for the local economy and provided jobs. These days it's hardly used. Perhaps that is a good thing. The risk of contamination increases with traffic. Any tanker that anchors at the port can potentially create an oil or gas spill. And then, you may have heard, they tried to launch this new project. Monster OilCorp was going to use explosives to construct their marine terminal off the island. Any explosions, even exploratory testing, endanger both the whales and the caves."

"Sarah told us that the marine terminal got overturned for environmental reasons."

"Yes, after months of protests. Perhaps *le Gardien* protected the island and the river from this latest threat."

"Le Gardien?" Deanna's eyes widened with interest.

"'The guardian of the caves.' It's a gigantic rock that looms over the cave entrance. It resembles a face. Actually, in Mi'gmaq creation tales, stones are animate beings—the bones of the earth, as it were. In the stories, sometimes shape-shifters appear as rocks, boulders, even cliffs ..."

Sarah nodded. She was thinking of the glacial rock in her garden.

"Amazing," exclaimed Deanna. "I've *got* to take some photos of le Gardien! But for that to happen, I'll have to convince Justin to actually let me come onto the island." She gave a pointed look at her boyfriend and said to him, "You know you still haven't shown me where you spend most of your waking hours! We've been here weeks already!"

"I told you, my supervisor's touchy about visitors coming on site. Not only that, she's expressly forbidden even us, the workers at the dig, from exploring the northern half of the island. She doesn't want us to find the ancient caves. It's crazy, I mean, I'd be super careful. I know they're sacred to the First Nations." He paused. "I hadn't realized until now just how passionate you were about visiting the island, Deanna. I'll make sure it happens." He put his arm around her.

"I have to leave in ten minutes for a party at my sister's house. Was there anything else you wanted to know?" Émile asked.

"Can you tell us a bit about the caves?" asked Deanna. "Have you had the chance to see the cave drawings yourself?"

"No, not me personally. But I met someone who was privileged to see them once, right after they were discovered, and that person sent me photos. But soon after that, an iron grill was installed to block the entrance—I guess to protect the drawings from curious intruders as well as to protect people who would otherwise try to explore the caves. It's real dangerous to go inside. Rocks shift around, could fall and badly injure—even kill—someone." He paused. "Like you, I was gripped with fascination. I remember meeting this visiting geologist, Bernadette, and having a drink with her in the village pub last year. Poor lady, I kept asking her questions about the caves!"

"What did she tell you?"

"She said she hadn't been able to find them though she'd looked. She explained to me about how the caves were formed—it was very interesting."

"And the drawings inside, did she tell you how old they are?" Deanna asked.

"She couldn't know since, like I said, she couldn't find the caves themselves. They're not so easy to find. Who knows? We're not even sure the cave paintings are genuine. Just possible some prankster drew stick figures on the cave wall to send people on a wild goose chase. The one time someone sent me photos, I emailed them to an expert. He and his colleagues visited Cacouna and took samples. They were going to carbon date the paint or pigments used and try to authenticate them. But I never heard back. That was years ago. Not a word since. I find it a bit odd that they never released the report."

"Maybe something's being covered up," said Justin.

"Who knows?" Émile shrugged. "Anyway, *bonne chance!* Hope your supervisor finally gives you the okay to look for the caves and check them out. If you can get past the bureaucracy and the iron grill, let me know what you discover." He winked at them as he got ready to go. "Just possible, you'll unearth buried treasure! Many shipwrecks occurred in the region. You never know what you'll stumble across. But be careful, remember, the rocks can shift at the slightest movement. Your lives are precious."

Around midnight, Matt stamped out the bonfire's embers to signal the end of the party. "Can I drive you guys home?" he offered Sarah.

She smiled gratefully. "Thanks. Bit late to walk back to the cottage. I didn't think this through. A ride would be welcome!"

Deanna leaned forward from the backseat of the car. "Justin can tell you that I suck at geography, Matt. So I'm confused: why do some locals refer to the island as a peninsula *and* others call it Gros-Cacouna Island? Is it an island or is it a peninsula? How can it be both?"

"Yup, it's confusing. Over many years, see, the strait between the island and the mainland has gradually turned into marshland. Much of the marsh is now mostly submerged in water, depending on the tides. Of course there's a road going out there now, on built-up land. I guess you could call the area a peninsula, but most people continue to call it Cacouna Island. Also, there's a huge rock just off the island, that's where many shipwrecks happened. It's called Cacouna Rock or *Petit Cacouna* (Little Cacouna). Hence, the island is *Gros-Cacouna* (Big Cacouna)."

"Wasaweg never mentions Petit Cacouna or Gros-Cacouna. I guess it was the French who came up with those names years later."

Matt glanced at her in the rear view mirror. "Ah, so you've been enjoying my ancestor's journal. I hoped you would."

"Yes! It's quite engrossing."

Sarah piped up: "She wouldn't put the book down. I had to confiscate it so she'd get out and about a bit. Speaking of which, Deanna, I think you'd love the bird sanctuary on the marshlands. I'll go with you on my day off if you want."

"Sure! And I'd *really* like to see where Justin works." Deanna had a gleam in her eye.

"You don't get up early enough to come with me," teased Justin. "You stay up reading until two or three every night. You're still in your pyjamas when the bus picks me up for work."

"I can drive you over any time later in the day," Matt offered. "Just phone me and I'll close the First Nation Centre for a couple of hours."

"That's kind of you. Hey! You're a longtime Cacouna resident, Matt. Could you pull any strings to help us get access to the caves so that we can explore them?"

"If your boyfriend works at the dig and isn't allowed, what can I do?"

"I just don't get it." Deanna looked glum. "Justin's team is helping excavate the old Mi'gmaq settlement. Why won't that professor what's-her-name give you guys permission to look for the caves?"

"Because Professor Jones is a total control freak." Justin scowled.

"She's got a secret agenda. *Something* is in those caves that she clearly doesn't want anyone else to know about," Deanna said.

"Like what?" Sarah asked.

"It can't be the cave drawings. When those kids stumbled into the caves a few years back, the paintings became public knowledge. Maybe Émile Beaulieu was onto something. Perhaps there *is* some local legend about stolen treasure stashed away in the caves? Just possible your supervisor got wind of the story."

"Whatever her reasons, she claims *she's* the only expert and only *she* can enter the caves. Any bets when we get off work for the Canada Day long weekend, she'll be scouring the caves all by herself next Saturday and Sunday!"

"So we'll beat her to it, right?" Deanna said.

"Absolutely." Justin nodded. "We'll postpone our trip to Tadoussac and the Saguenay River. Instead, we'll sneak over to the area where we think the caves are and locate them. We'll go next Friday night. That gives us a week to plan it."

"I dunno," Sarah said.

"I *do* know. What you're suggesting is a punishable violation of the law," said Matt sternly. "The iron bars were installed to keep people out. I'm going to pretend I didn't hear this conversation." A moment later, with a mischievous grin, he said, "But if you need a driver, I'm available."

# ELEVEN: MOVING THE SACRED GLACIAL STONE

Deanna rocked back and forth in the old pine rocker near the fireplace. Sarah puttered around in the kitchen, cleaning up after dinner. Justin had already retired to the attic bedroom. Deanna tried not to think about Wasaweg's diary. Ever since her friends had suggested, a few days earlier, that she stop reading it, she had felt all the more drawn to finish the story. She tried to focus instead on the first paragraphs of her essay for her literature class, but the papers lay limply in her lap. She picked up a section and noted a few sentences that could be tweaked. She crossed out a few words and added a couple of sentences. *Much better.* She read the revised paragraphs out loud. "Chapter Three: The Wandering Academician. Both Novalis and George MacDonald feature a student-hero, who, for some time, wanders away from academia and into fantastical realms where extraordinary adventures take place. By means of travel and visionary dreams, the youth leaves behind his intellectual upbringing that was shaped by society and college. MacDonald's novel *Lilith* opens with the main character, Mr. Vane, deep in study in the well-supplied library of his house, unconscious of the fact that he is about to embark on a fantastic adventure. In *Heinrich von Ofterdingen,* a novel by Novalis, we read that the protagonist 'became lost in sweet fantasies' and 'dreamed of boundless distances and wild, unknown regions. ... traversed seas ... lived with many kinds of people.'" The last line about 'wild, unknown regions' made her remember Wasaweg's manuscript. She put her essay down on a side table and tiptoed over to the pine cabinet. *Could Sarah have hidden it in here?* She opened the smallest drawer where the Beaumont family kept the silverware. She glanced around to see if anyone was looking. She couldn't help herself; she felt inexplicably drawn to this story; it had become an obsession. At the back of the drawer, behind a pair of silver ladles, was a blue folder. She pulled it out. Sarah had slipped the manuscript inside. Deanna returned the empty folder to the drawer, but tucked the journal under her arm. She plunked herself in the rocking chair and opened the manuscript to where she'd left off reading.

*Wasaweg's Diary*

*Kakoua-Nak Island, 1690*

The next night, we beat our drums: the timeless rhythm—Mother Earth's heartbeat. We danced beneath the moon, preparing to move the ancient stone from the centre of our village on the island to the mainland. Clouds gathered and swirled in the evening sky. Diane seemed almost tipsy and sat unusually close to Matthieu on a huge piece of driftwood, set apart from the bonfire where people had begun gathering for the celebration. Neither of them saw me as I crouched in the shadows of the trees to collect more twigs for the fire.

"Here's for good luck," Diane whispered to my husband. She hung a slender gold cord with a shell around his neck. "I found it on the beach when I first arrived on the island. I want you to have it before I leave. I hope it protects you."

"You're going somewhere?" He was shocked, just as I had been when she had broken the news to me.

"Yes, soon I will leave, and we won't see one another again, not in this lifetime. I pray to God I will see you again." She kissed him on the cheek.

"Why would you leave us after living as part of our family for these past years? The children see you as their auntie. They'll be devastated. Wasaweg, too. She loves you like a sister."

"Do *you* love me as a sister, Matthieu?"

"Of course."

"I *am* your sister, but you forgot me. In another lifetime, more than three centuries from now, we live on the Island of Montreal. In that life, my name is Deanna and yours is Matthew. Our surname is Aynsworth."

"An English name? I'm not English, too, I hope!" He laughed. I could tell he was humouring her and didn't believe a word she uttered, although I, strangely, did.

"Yes, we were both brought up in an English family. You think I'm joking. I'm not. English and French live side by side in the future; theirs are the two official languages of our country—Canada."

"Canada? What kind of name is that?" he joked. "And tell me, if the English and French become allies, what will happen to the First People of the land?"

"Only now, after being treated abysmally by Europeans, are First Nations' rights, cultures, and languages finally being recognized, bit by bit, but it hardly makes up for the incredible losses they suffered over five centuries of oppression and abuse."

For a moment, he looked on the verge of believing her story. Then he burst out: "Five centuries! Why, Jacques Cartier arrived on these shores fewer than two hundred years ago! What an imagination you have, Diane! How you spin tall tales! No wonder you entertain the children! But you don't seem to be yourself tonight. You speak the way a drunkard or a madwoman does."

Diane's voice was filled with sadness. "No, every word I say is true. You and I will one day grow up as brother and sister. You don't remember it in your waking hours. But in your dreams, I know you still remember us, your other family. I've heard you talking in your sleep— mumbling about experiences we share in that other life. You even reached out to communicate to me once in a dream—across the centuries. You mock me, but I'm telling you the truth before I leave." She put her hand on his arm. "Matthew, I was hoping you'd come with me."

I stiffened and the hair on the back of my neck stood on end though the night was warm.

"Why are you speaking so strangely, Diane? Are you ill?" Matthieu felt her forehead for fever, then patted her on the head as if she were a sick child. "You'll move to the mainland with us and enjoy happy days in our new home. All will be well, I promise."

The sinking stone in my heart told me that Diane would not yield. A cold shadow hovered over me. I felt scared she would not only depart, but take Matthieu with her, too. And if they left, my children would cry and so would I, though I'd hide my tears, try to be strong for my young family. I would weep and weep, for no man could fill the void Matthieu would leave behind—he was, and forever is, my soul mate.

The celebrations began, and people started chanting and dancing. We feasted on harvested squash, roasted corn and other grains, and some folk smoked the sacred tobacco, and we prayed. We retold our ancestors' stories. We felt their presence in the flames of the bonfire and we saw their visions in the blue shadows between the flames. Hours passed. I slept.

When I opened my eyes, the full moon was shining brightly, illuminating the ground around us. She was partway through her slow dance across the dark sky. I smelled the sweet-smelling herbs Lentug had cast on the embers of the fire. Our sacred rock had vanished, leaving only a deep imprint on the ground where it had lain for millennia.

Clan members lay sleeping on the ground, babies in their mothers' arms, wives in the arms of their partners. A deep peace pervaded the night. The stars shone bright in the sky. I reached out to touch my little children as they slept—the length of a raccoon's tail from me—blissfully in my husband's strong, protective arms. Suddenly, a loud explosion rocked the island. A smell of acrid smoke reached us. An unseen enemy fired canon after canon. The earth shook beneath our fragile bodies.

"Quick! Race toward the caves on the other side of the island!" Lentug yelled. He grabbed our elderly father and put him on his back and carried Mother in his arms. He began to run, for he was strong and fast as the wind.

Matthieu scooped up our daughter and son with one arm and shook me with his free hand. "Wasaweg, don't just stand there wide-eyed! We've *got* to leave! The Redcoats are attacking!"

Stunned, I watched my body move as if I were watching it from far, far away. I darted into our wigwam and grabbed a basket of fruit and a pouch of medicinal herbs. Émilie picked up our blankets and we caught up to Matthieu, racing barefoot beside him, alongside all the fleeing members of our small community. We moved through cover of night and crossed the rough terrain toward the secret, sacred caves where we knew we would find shelter.

We reached them before dawn. The three caves were interconnected. At the back of the second cave, through a low archway, lay a third, hidden cavern, barely big enough for our few families to hide in. After we crowded into it, I leaned over and whispered to Diane, "You can join the English camp if you want to save your life. Tell them you were kidnapped by us. You wanted to leave, anyway."

It was the only time I ever saw her really angry. Her eyes darkened. She glowered at me and whispered, "I'm not proud of what the Europeans have done to the First People of this beautiful country! Don't you know that by now, Wasaweg? I consider you, Matthieu, and your children to be my own family."

"Then why are you leaving us?" I turned my face from her. Tears slipped down my cheeks. I kept my sobs in check. The children had finally fallen asleep. But I knew in my gut that my world had ended. Now I saw that Lentug had been right all along. We had no choice except to leave our blessed island, the land of our ancestors. After a few minutes, I felt Diane reach out to me in the dark. She wiped my tears away. "It'll be all right, Wasaweg. You'll survive this. I am sure of it."

After a few hours, we ventured out of the innermost cavern back into the second cave. It seemed roomy by comparison. Every time the distant echo of canons erupted, we'd retreat and huddle, just in case the English might chance to find our hideout. For three long days and nights, we lived inside the caves, surviving on berries, wild cherries, rosehips, and other foods we had brought or could find nearby. Émilie told jokes, for she was a cheerful girl by nature, and Diane told us crazy tales that she made-up—about flying machines that travelled over the earth like big, metal birds with wide, silver wings. What fantastical stories she invented! She kept the children busy and entertained so that they wouldn't know what a terrible situation we were actually in.

One morning she asked them to draw a picture of our village as they remembered it. Matthis doesn't like colouring, he's too young, but Isabelle took out coloured paints Diane had given her. On a small thin piece of dried birch bark, Isabelle mapped out all the paths and wigwams, the site of the sacred well, and the location of the ancient sacred rock that had rested on Cacouna Island for thousands of years—long before we ever came to live on it—until that fateful night, the eve of the English invasion, when we moved the rock to the mainland.

After my daughter had finished sketching, Diane rolled up the birch bark sketch and went to the mural in the second cave.

Only three weeks earlier, Diane and I had visited the sacred caves. We had added our own drawings to the large mural in the middle cave: she had drawn a seal and I had painted a star-flower directly above the seal's eyes.

The children were busy playing with Émilie while Lentug and Matthieu talked in low voices by the fire. As Diane and I stood before the mural once more, I noticed her eyeing the small but deep crack in the rock next to my star flower. We looked at one another and nodded. An unspoken agreement had passed between us. With the tip of her knife, she chipped a little deeper into the crack. Then she rolled up Isabelle's map tightly and tucked it into the hole. I took out the paints and added longer petals to the star flower above the seal's eyes so that it would now mask the hole in the mural. We smiled at one another. "Mission accomplished," Diane said.

"Yes. And Lentug and Matthieu never even noticed what we were doing! They're too busy drawing up plans for the new home!"

The next day, I noticed my brother seemed unduly thoughtful. At first I thought it was because he was concerned about our imminent departure. Then I realized that something else was eating at him. I saw him glance over at Diane several times, giving her a look I'd never seen before in his eyes. It was clear that Lentug was in love with her.

"You're going to leave us?" he was saying to Diane in a whisper. "After all that we've been through together! Why on earth?" he asked. He reached out and touched her hand.

"I'm sorry. I, I belong—" she stumbled for words. "I need to go back to someone. My family, my—"

Lentug was a healer and a visionary, but he could be as human as anyone else. "You're married?" he asked, shocked and angry, pulling his hand back.

"No. No! Not yet. But … It's complicated. I don't belong to this time. You've had visions, Lentug. I know you have—I've seen your sketches. Maybe you don't know it, but much of what you draw belongs to another time in history. My time. The twenty-first century. Perhaps your visions are glimpses of the future—shadowy memories of things you will one day experience in a future incarnation. Or maybe it's like when great visionary artists draw things that get invented years later."

"I'm surprised to hear you speak of reincarnation; you're a Christian. Anyway, even if you and I never meet again in another lifetime, we'll at least reunite in the celestial realm."

"We will see one another in *this world,* Lentug, but not in this era. I am sure of it. I've seen sketches of myself in your drawings of that future time; I haven't figured out why yet …" She reached out and took his hand. The firelight flickered across his high cheekbones and illuminated his dark eyes, which had filled with sadness and shadows.

"No matter. I kept quiet all these months, waiting … I'm sorry I even spoke of this."

"Don't be sorry, Lentug—"

Then she said something I couldn't hear, because I got distracted by Matthis who had started crying. I had to comfort and soothe my boy, even more so now that there was the possibility that some of the English soldiers had strayed over to our little corner of the island.

At last, the sound of the canons exploding stopped beating against our eardrums. From a distance, we heard the rough, foreign voices of the invaders retreating over the water in their boats. Finally the air was calm and it was safe to leave the caves. I knew the soldiers would return with their womenfolk and children to settle—or destroy—our island, Great Spirit's island. But for the moment, we had some breathing space.

Our last day on Kakoua-Nak Island was bittersweet, but mainly bitter. *Wapg,* the dawn light, irradiated the burgeoning, rose-coloured clouds that filled the sky like flowers. The beauty struck my heart with soft arrows. The day had arrived that we must leave our beautiful island, the gift of our ancestors. The three other families who had hidden out with us in the caves set off to see what, if anything, remained of our village. They hoped the invaders would not return and had decided to stay on the island. I believed we would never see the villagers again. For though our future was uncertain, of one thing I was sure, the foreigners would return to claim the island for the Europeans.

Our family marched along the beach to the *pewisg* (a small canoe) that Lentug had kept hidden near the shore.

"*Witu'lumua?*" asked little Matthis. He had just learned this word; it meant "to go in the same canoe."

Lentug replied, "No, your father and I will swim." Because, you see, all of us couldn't fit in the canoe, not even with the children in our laps.

"I'll swim," said Diane. "Matthieu can go with the children–I'm a strong swimmer. Or I can go another day; you can come back for me."

"No, women, children, and elders first," Matthieu said gallantly. He helped my parents and the children into the canoe. Émilie and I followed.

Diane refused to enter it. She sat on a big boulder on the beach with an undecipherable expression on her face. "I'll be fine," she kept saying. "Just go. Matthieu must take my place in the canoe. It's only right. You must travel together as a family. If you want, come back for me tomorrow or the day after. I'll be fine for a day or two. Plenty of fruit left."

But my husband wouldn't acquiesce to her and I, too, did not yield. I placed my paddle across my knees. "We won't leave unless you come with us," I declared. "You were already planning on leaving for the mainland before the English attacked. I don't get it, why won't you travel with us?"

Finally, although unwilling, Diane relented. Matthieu helped her into the canoe. Then he leaned over and kissed me—a sweet, lingering kiss. He gave each of the children a hug. Lentug had already begun swimming, so Matthieu waded up to his thighs in water and pushed the canoe out into the current. He waved cheerfully. "Don't worry, my love. I'll see you in a few hours."

"Papa!" Isabelle cried out as we sped away. "Papa, Papa! Don't forget us, not even for a moment. Swim like a seal! We love you!"

All went well; not that far into our journey, Diane stood up in the canoe. To my horror, she slipped out of her moccasins and plunged into the water. It happened so fast I couldn't stop her without risking us capsizing the canoe, for I was at the stern, steering with my paddle. My body trembled from head to toe as I watched her swim with swift strokes back the way we'd come.

Stunned, I stared at her retreating figure; it got smaller and smaller, and, as the form slipped further away from us, it appeared to me that Diane had been like a bright comet in our lives and was now merely the tiniest pinpoint of a star in the darkening sky. Finally, she disappeared, invisible in the blue-black waves—like when you go deep underwater with open eyes and see no differences between water or earth or sky. Tears trickled down my face. I brushed them aside and began to sing a chant my great-grandmother had taught me. I had to be strong for the children. I couldn't mar my face with tracks of sorrow. I would welcome Matthieu and Lentug at our new home with a bright smile and eyes full of hope. I refused to succumb to regret for all we had willingly or unwillingly left behind on Cacouna Island.

On the mainland, Bernard Beaumont, the young farmer Lentug had befriended, was waiting for us, a strong seventeen-year-old with a freckled face. He greeted us warmly. Lentug had arranged the meeting days before; he had planned that we would journey to the new homestead a few days after the ceremony of moving the great rock. I knew now that Lentug had been right all along. Just a few weeks earlier, he had prophesied, "Our time here has ended. Any day the English will invade this sanctuary." I had been wrong to resist moving. Now

I thanked the stars that my brother had the gift of vision. His foresight and acumen had saved us.

Bernard's kindness to us was like sunshine after heavy rains. He helped my parents get out of the canoe, then my children, and finally Émilie and me. Then he lifted each of us, one by one, even the cat, onto his hay wagon. The children stopped crying when he handed them each an apple to eat. They burst out laughing when he started juggling the rest of the apples. *He's a good lad,* I thought as I settled in next to him on the wagon seat. He let me grip the reins and steer the horses for the second half of the wagon journey toward our new home, about five kilometres upriver from where we had come ashore.

We bumped along a dirt track and pulled into a clearing in a wood. Through the trees we could faintly hear the sound of the waves on the shore—we were up a steep incline from the beach below. "This is my farm," he said, pointing to a tilled field next to the woods. "The forest over there is yours. Your brother, Lentug, purchased it from me last week. We share a path to the beach and river."

Flanked on either side by my elderly parents, I stepped onto our new land. Isabelle hung onto my back, her small hands wrapped around my neck, and Émilie cradled little Matthis in her arms. When we put the children down and looked around, we saw that the glacial rock rested in the centre of the forest clearing. Great Spirit's sentinel, the Rock, had been waiting for us to arrive—mysteriously transported there the night of our ceremony on the island, as we slept around the embers of our bonfire, after our hours of chanting songs about the creation of the world—those ancient tales we pass on to each new generation. It seemed so long ago now—before the Redcoats had wracked the quiet of the night with their fireballs and chaos.

Over what remained of the day, my parents, Émilie, Isabelle and I constructed a makeshift shelter. Bernard, the young farmer, helped us, and brought us food to eat. I knew that Matthieu and Lentug would build something more enduring, but we needed a roof over our heads for the night. The men would be exhausted from their swim and trek. The children were worn out, especially Matthis, so I put them to bed early. They fell asleep next to Émilie on the fragrant balsam boughs we had spread on the dirt floor of our new home. I rested beside them and listened to the sound of their breathing and my parents' snoring. I saw—through the entrance of our lean-to—the stars appear and fill the sky.

I waited and waited for my brother and husband to arrive. I could see more stars than darkness, so bright they were, and it seemed like a good omen—a clear night resplendent with the heavens' lights.

I couldn't sleep. After hours of waiting, I felt restless. I left the shelter to sit by the big rock. The moon shone crisp and clear against the starlit ebony sky. Seals howled on the reefs. I remembered Diane and hoped she had made it back to the island safely. I knew she was a good swimmer. My initial shock had worn off and I was more angry at her than worried. *What a thing to do!*

In the quiet of the night, waves crashed against the shore below. At last, Lentug appeared at the top of the forest path that ascended from the beach. His clothes were sopping wet, and his face, in the moonlight, was creviced with lines of sadness. I burst into tears. He had arrived alone. I knew. Matthieu, my beloved, was gone.

Earlier, I had lit a fire next to the big rock. I handed my brother my blanket and he crouched down near the campfire. He avoided my eyes. "Tell me, brother..." I began. My words ended there.

He shivered. "After we watched the canoe move toward the mainland, I felt sure you would reach the other side in good time. You rode the current and the wind blew in your favour. So I began swimming. I was a few metres out and glanced back, thinking Matthieu must be directly behind me. Instead, he was still standing, ankle-deep in water, by the beach. He yelled, 'Go ahead, Lentug! I'm coming in now!' I'm a healer, Wasaweg. I have visions, premonitions. I should have known better. Why didn't I wait for him?"

I couldn't speak a word. As the flashflood so often follows the first spring thaw, so doubt inundated me. Worries crammed my mind: *Perhaps not all soldiers had left the island. One of them could have grabbed Matthieu on the beach. What if he's been kidnapped by the English, or worse? What if he started swimming and got a leg cramp ... The river water is freezing!* A cold, disheartening realization began to dawn on me. *In the past seven years, I never saw Matthieu swim. Not once. He loved to canoe, but he never actually went into the water. How could I not have put two and two together and realized that Matthieu was not a good swimmer? I should have protected him ...* Then anger and regret surfaced. *We lost everything trying to save that strange, foreign woman so that she would go with us to the mainland. And she didn't even want to come! Why did we coerce her?* I couldn't even utter her name in my mind; I was so angry and hurt. And then grief engulfed me. Tears and tears fell down. In one day, I had lost Matthieu, my beloved, and Diane, my best friend. Lentug wept with me. He had lost both his brother-in-law and the woman he loved unrequitedly. He and I crouched by the fire beside our great protector, the ancient glacial rock. We cried like the waves pounding the shore and the seals moaning on the reef.

Just before dawn, I crawled into the lean-to and went to lie down, exhausted, beside my children. I hoped that when I woke up the bad dream would be gone and Matthieu, my children's father, would be home in our arms. I hung the dream-catcher over their sleeping heads. But the dream-catcher didn't work.

We never found my husband's body. He had vanished. Sometimes I wonder if Diane whisked him away to wherever she had come from. Only Great Spirit knows. Moment-to-moment I pray to see him again.

# TWELVE: THE HIDDEN MURAL

Deanna closed the manuscript. *Without a doubt, Wasaweg's husband, Matthieu Landry, is my own brother, Matthew,* she thought. *Matthew somehow slipped back in time when he stared at that painting and returned to a life he had once lived in New France. And that means I was Diane,* she realized with a gasp, *the foreign woman whom Wasaweg describes in her journal.* Even as the revelation sank in, a doubt arose in Deanna's mind. *If I succeeded in travelling back in time, then why isn't Matthew home? Have I already travelled back in time but failed to persuade him to return to life in our century? Is it like that old movie, 'Groundhog Day,' where the main character keeps getting stuck in a loop, repeating the same day over and over again, trying to resolve his problem but failing again and again? Even if I go back, there's no guarantee I can change the past and get Matthieu to leave with me this time.* She sucked in her breath. She had no choice. She didn't like the idea of going back in time, because of the danger that she could get stuck in another era. She pictured her parents' faces, grief-constricted as when Matthew had gone missing. She couldn't possibly put them through that again. Then she breathed out. She imagined her father's eyes glistening with joy as he hugged his son. She *had* to try to get her brother back. Whether or not this was her first or second attempt at going back in time, it didn't really matter. Deanna was adamant—her new life mission was to convince Matthieu Landry to leave New

France with her—through the portal in the Cacouna caves that she was sure existed—so that he could resume his life as Matthew Aynsworth in the twenty-first century. This would be the only way to save him from drowning in the Saint Lawrence River or perhaps dying at the point of a bayonet on the island. She had to give it her best shot. *If I don't try,* she thought, *not only will Wasaweg have lost Matthieu forever, I, too, will never see my brother Matthew again.*

\*\*\*

It was Friday night and the eve of Canada's national holiday. Justin's supervisor had told everyone to leave work at noon and take the rest of the long weekend off. Matt, Sarah, Justin and Deanna decided to cross over to the island and look for the caves after an early supper, as the tide would be low enough that evening to access the caves if they timed it right.

The road from the mainland to Cacouna Island zigzagged across the eastern half of the island. A sign "forbidden access" prevented them from driving any further. They backtracked a bit and tried another road that also was on private land. They passed the abandoned farmhouse where Father Louis Stevenart and his dozen orphans had tried to raise geese one winter long ago, in 1898. They drove further and passed a dozen or so houses.

"If anyone asks you, we're visiting Pierre's cousin, okay? His family owns a cottage here," Matt said. He parked the car at the end of the road well out of sight of the last private home. The first thing he did once he got out of the car was slip his car keys under a flat rock and roll a log over it. "In case something happens to me inside the caves. You never know. At least someone else will be able to drive everyone back."

"Sounds ominous," Sarah said.

"You've gotta be prepared for any eventuality. We're all taking a big risk."

They began walking in a westerly direction over big rocks covered in green algae. "Careful!" Matt grabbed Sarah's arm as she began to slide. Justin was marching on ahead.

Deanna trailed behind her friends. As she walked, a shiny object in a little pool of water caught her eye. A thumb-sized white seashell hung from a glittering, golden necklace. Someone had carefully threaded the fine chain through a hole in the shell. She lingered, gazing at it. The others walked far ahead, their forms getting smaller by the minute. She hesitated. *Damn shoelaces.* She crouched to tie her laces tighter, still staring at the necklace. It glinted like a jewel in the water. *Could this be the same necklace Diane gave Matthieu on the night the Mi'gmaq moved the glacial rock? Did the ornament wash ashore after he drowned? What if I pick it up and bring it with me into the past, will I be that Diane—the woman who caused the necklace to be described in Wasaweg's diary? I must reach them in time and try and coax my brother to get into the canoe instead of me. He was always a terrible swimmer ... When he was a little kid, he freaked out in the swimming pool.* All these thoughts flashed through her mind in seconds. She reached into the pool of water and grabbed the gold chain and its white shell. Then she sprang up and sprinted ahead, trying to catch up to the group.

When she caught up with the others, Justin was looking up at the cliffs and asking Matt questions about the caves. "Who discovered them?"

"They've been around forever," Matt answered. "We all grew up hearing about them. No one's really encouraged to walk on this half of the island. When we were kids, at least once a summer, we'd manage to sneak across from the mainland at low tide and we'd sometimes dare one other to race up the beach to le Gardien. But it was all bluff and no action. We never actually found le Gardien or the caves, right, Sarah?"

"Right. We heard rumours. Granny tales. For a kid, stories about le Gardien are just like believing a pirate lives on Cacouna Rock. Exciting and scary. But when you grow up, you think they're made-up stories such as believing in Santa Claus. I was floored when I heard that two kids had actually stumbled into the caves and discovered ancient drawings. It was all over the local news for a while, but after a while the story was buried in other news and forgotten."

"Clearly, the caves are not easily discoverable or accessible," said Justin. "I mean, other people would have found them too; and le Gardien—that sounds like it should be easy to find, but you guys looked when you were kids and didn't find anything. And we should be in the general vicinity but we haven't seen anything."

"It's dusk. It's not easy to scope anything out right now," pointed out Deanna.

"Well," said Sarah, "Émile Beaulieu warned us that boulders might shift around and fall down inside the caves. I don't think we should go inside even if we do luck out and find them. We can just peer in using our flashlights."

A half hour later, Matt declared the search over. "We'll never find them now that it's almost dark."

He and Sarah turned around and began walking back in the direction of the car.

"Can't just give up like this!" Deanna hissed to Justin. "I'm not leaving without finding those caves. They've got to be here somewhere."

He put his arms around her and hugged her tightly. "I'm disappointed, too."

"What about up there?" She directed the beam of her flashlight over his shoulder. The light flashed upward to the right and focused on a tall oblong rock. "Oh my God! What luck! See the aquiline nose and the eyes? That must be le Gardien! It's like he's been standing here for millennia, watching over the beach and the river."

"Well, if that's him, then the caves are nearby, too! Let me go ahead and check it out," said Justin. Within minutes, he shouted down. "She's right. This is it! Watch your step. The path up is really steep!"

As they approached, they could clearly see the semblance of eyes, a nose, and a mouth, carved out by the ravages of time. Ochre-coloured lichens further defined the face's mysterious features.

Matt, overcome by emotion and reverence, said in a choked up voice, *"Le Gardien des grottes*—the guardian of the caves."

Beneath the protective shadow of le Gardien, the entrance to the first cave was half veiled by a lone spruce tree. The entrance itself was barred by a rusty iron gate closed with a small padlock. Beyond it the walls of the cave rose up within the rock face.

Matt turned and faced each of his companions. "Are you sure you want to enter?"

Justin stepped forward and broke off the lock with a pair of bolt cutters and swung open the iron gate that sealed the entrance. One by one, they filed in.

The first cave was spacious—about five metres by seven metres, and at least ten metres high. Ten or fifteen people could fit in it easily. "No sand in here. So the tide never reaches this high up," Justin noted.

Sarah shone her flashlight on the far wall. "Cave paintings!"

They saw first a faded drawing of two humans standing beside a small animal. The taller human was holding a weapon.

Justin stepped back from the wall to get perspective. "If these drawings are authentic, then the fact that the guy in the picture's wielding a javelin and not a bow and arrow indicates these drawings were done in the Middle Woodlands period."

"Not all of us are academics, Justin. Ordinary English please. When was the Middle Woodlands period?" Deanna asked.

"Between 1000 to 2500 BC."

"Do you think maybe the First People drew them?" Matt asked.

"No clue," said Sarah. "They could just as easily have been done by a kid fifty years ago. They have yet to be authenticated."

"No, no! The drawings were here back in 1690! The Mi'gmaq knew about them," Deanna interjected.

"How can you be sure?" Sarah asked.

"Wasaweg described them in her journal. I was reading all about it last night."

"But you said you'd stopped reading her diary—after that day on the beach when you had the nightmare." Justin shot her a concerned look.

"It wasn't a nightmare. It was a dream of Matthew, though it *was* pretty weird that he appeared to me as a seal. The only bad thing about it was waking up and not knowing more. It was like getting just part of a text message—with the main part missing. And about Wasaweg's manuscript, I'm sorry, I confess—I read until four this morning. I just couldn't get rest until I finished reading it." She looked down to avoid Sarah's gaze.

Sarah chuckled. "So that was you in the living room in the wee hours. I thought it was a little mouse that had snuck into the cupboard and was rummaging through the family silverware looking for bread crumbs."

"You're not angry?"

"Forgiven." Sarah smiled. "But, since you've finished reading Wasaweg's journal, why not lend it to Justin? After all, he's the one excavating the Mi'gmaq settlement ruins. It might offer him some insights."

"Matt should decide what to do with the diary. Here, I have it on me. I was meaning to return it to you, Matt. Pierre said he'll borrow it from you later as he's too busy to read it right now." Deanna reached into her bag and handed Matt the manuscript.

"Sarah's right," Matt said. "I agree that Justin should have a chance to read it before I take it back to the First Nation Centre." He passed the diary to Justin who slipped it into his knapsack. "Okay. Now that we're actually in here, let's take some photos. This is awesome!" He pulled out his digital camera.

Everyone turned back to study the paintings.

"You know, guys, Wasaweg's and Matthieu's family and friends hid in here for a few days," Deanna said after several minutes, breaking the lull in conversation. "They were hiding from the English. The soldiers had launched a cannon attack on the island, you see. I'm pretty sure it was the last place Matthieu—Matthew—stayed before he disappeared from New France. I'm positive he would have left a sign or message for me inside one of the three caves."

Before they could stop her, she had ducked under the low arch that led into the next cave.

"There's a third cave? I only heard about two," Matt said. "Does anyone know what the hell she's talking about? What kind of message could she possibly expect to receive from her missing brother?"

"She believes her brother is the reincarnation of Matthieu Landry," Sarah explained. "Or, to put it another way, she thinks that in a previous life, Matthew Aynsworth was Matthieu Landry."

"Wow, Deanna's really losing it," said Matt.

"Hey!" Justin said protectively. "Her brother went missing. It's hard enough to accept when someone dies, but to *not* know what happened, never have any closure, must be agony. I'm actually surprised she's done as well as she has. I don't know how *I* would have managed. I think we can give her some leeway if her line between reality and fantasy is a bit blurry right now."

"In here!" Deanna shouted from the second cave. "You've got to see this! It's unbelievable!"

The others raced in to join her in the second cave. Red ochre paint on one cave wall depicted two children playing on a beach. A seal stretched comfortably out on a large rock. The North Shore mountains loomed across the river.

"The seal's sunbathing," Sarah said. "They do that, you know. I often see the same seal when I walk on the beach. For years now it's been coming around: it swims in on sunny days and lies on the big rock directly beneath the gazebo to bask in the sun. When high tide comes in, it swims out to join its clan, I guess."

"Something unusual about this one," Justin said. "His eyes follow you wherever you turn." He walked a few paces to the left and glanced at the drawing again. "Yup. Still staring at me."

"Don't you see!" Deanna burst out. "Sarah, this is the same creature that your ancestor, Wasaweg, depicted, you know, the one in the weaving that hangs over the—"

"You're kidding, right, Deanna?" Matt interrupted. "I appreciate your enthusiasm, but don't you think it's a fairly commonplace scene? I mean, all seals look alike. After all, they're native to the lower Saint Lawrence region. Until a few decades ago, the Saint Lawrence River teemed with them. So why *wouldn't* the people who lived in the caves represent them in their art?"

"I agree with Deanna," Sarah piped up. "The creature's eyes are almost human. And just above his eyes, he has a distinct mark—a star-shaped flower—just like the one in Wasaweg's weaving."

Deanna stepped closer to the wall. "You can see that the seal is clearly defined. Also, the paint isn't faded as with the other drawings. You know, I think someone added the seal to the mural much later on. I wonder why."

"I'm beginning to think these cave drawings are genuinely old," said Sarah. "Modern people may not be able to grasp what the artists were communicating, but I'm sure that everything portrayed in this mural has symbolic meaning. The people who drew these images, the First People, my ancestors, dreamed true dreams—visions. Their tales, passed down orally, were based on intuitive wisdom. The First Nations had an evolved culture—tuned in to the stars and planets, and even other universes." She glanced at Deanna. "I believe this is one of those supernatural power spots—portals to other realms—that I was telling you about back at the cottage the other day. Our rational minds can't comprehend them, but the power points exist—far realer than what we think is real."

And just as Sarah uttered the word "real," the wall began to move.

"Let's get out of here," said Justin, stepping back. He eyed new cracks in the cave. "The structure of these caves is quite unsound. I hate to admit it, but Professor Jones was right. We shouldn't have entered in here." The earth shook again, harder this time. "Earthquake! Get out!" he yelled.

Sarah was out first, but only because Matt had shoved her toward the cave's entrance. She stumbled and regained her footing on the other side of the archway. "Hurry!" she yelled as she raced out into the open air. He followed and a moment later, a chunk of the stone ceiling crashed down, along with a big boulder, and completely blocked the entrance to the middle cave.

"My God!" she gasped. They shone the flashlight toward the second cave and saw that an enormous boulder now divided them from their friends.

"Justin! Deanna!" Matt shouted.

"Can you hear us?" Sarah yelled. Complete silence engulfed them. A wall of stone had trapped their friends inside. Stunned, Matt dragged his feet as he moved away from the cave entrance. Small rocks continued falling. Ashen-faced, Sarah followed him robotically. Tears trickled down her cheeks. She stopped and tried her cell phone. "Not working. We've got to go get help."

When they finally reached the car, he kicked the log away and grabbed the car keys. "I'll drive straight to the village fire station. A rescue team will get to work on saving Deanna and Justin. I'm sure they're alive." But the tone in his voice belied the confidence he tried to project. He gripped the steering wheel and slammed the accelerator. "They have to be," he grunted.

Sarah clutched her stomach as the vehicle tore off. Each remained alone with their thoughts until they reached the village.

# THIRTEEN: SLIPPING BACK IN TIME

## THE MOVING MURAL

Deanna and Justin crouched by the wall. "If that was an earthquake," said Justin, "we could experience aftershocks. Let's be as still as possible and hope the debris settles. No doubt, Sarah and Matt have already left to find help."

Deanna leaned in and gave him a lingering kiss. "I love you," she said softly.

"I love you, too." He gingerly stood up and offered her a hand, pulling her close. For a long time they held each other. "Don't cry, Deanna. We've got to stay strong and remain hopeful until the rescue team arrives."

She had just lifted her head from his shoulder and was about to reply, when she stopped, her attention riveted on the mural. "Justin! Look at the writing on the wall! Do you see the signature and date inscribed below the painting of the seal?"

He turned around and glanced. "I see a squiggly line. It's the artist's simplistic attempt at drawing a wave."

"No, no! Don't you see! He did that deliberately to mask his inscription. Here—" She craned her head forward. "Give me your flashlight."

He handed it to her. "How do you know it's a *he* who did the doodle?"

"See, Matthew etched his name beneath the seal's flipper. I'd recognize his signature anywhere."

"Okay …" he said doubtfully and peered at the lines.

"See for yourself." She shone the light on the seal. "*Matthew, 1690.* It's starting to come back to me now. I remember we hid a scroll right behind the image of the flower."

"Wasaweg's diary has pulled you into her story so deep, now you're even identifying with one of the characters. This was why we advised you to put away the manuscript—it's too close to home for you. Both you and Wasaweg lost someone you loved. Neither of you got closure."

"I'm not just a character in the story! This isn't me being over imaginative!" she said indignantly. "Ever since the earthquake, I see everything crystal clear. And don't think it's because I read in her journal! You of all people know the difference between just reading about something and living it. Isn't that why you wanted to work hands on at a real, archaeological site rather than simply reading academic textbooks? I'm telling you, Justin, *I'm* the one who stuffed a drawing inside the wall of this cave."

"You did *what*? Are you crazy? So you're saying you've actually been in here before?" He shot her an incredulous look.

"At some point in time—I'm still unsure if it already happened or if it's about to happen. But yes, I know these caves inside out. I get it now—why the manuscript drew me in like that, why the Cacouna Island caves fascinated me and I had to come and see them for myself, it all begins to make sense—" she began.

Justin interjected, "Not to me, Deanna. I'm worried about you. During the earthquake you must have hit your head. Here." He waved his index finger back and forth in front of her eyes. "Follow my finger."

"Come on, Justin," she said. "I don't have a concussion. I'm fine. But I'm getting pretty annoyed by all your doubts." She stepped forward and tapped the mural with her fingernail. Dry bits of the painted-on flower flaked off.

"Are you nuts? Do you want to trigger a total collapse of the cave?"

She laughed. "Scraping my fingernail against the wall isn't going to cause another earthquake. And stop calling me crazy! I'm not!"

Justin squinted and stepped closer to the wall. "A piece of paper *is* sticking out ..." He carefully extracted a thin roll of birch bark from the hole which had, until Deanna tapped the surface, been covered by the star-shaped flower. "You might be onto something. Someone *did* deliberately hide this—whatever it is—behind the mural." He unfurled the birch bark. "A map. Damn, you were right! How did you know? How awesome! It's a detailed drawing of the old Mi'gmaq village."

She leaned in. "It's better than a blueprint: it depicts the hidden paths, where everything stood, and what the wigwams looked like, even what people wore in those days. It shows the precise location of the communal well and the site of the ancient stone, the glacial rock they considered sacred."

"The artist had a childlike style of drawing, but hey, this will help enormously with the dig! Oh, here's a signature at the end—Isabelle."

"Wasaweg's daughter. She was six at the time. She had been forced to stay inside the caves for three days with her family, hiding out from English soldiers. I bet she was bored out of her tree, you know, the way kids get when they can't go and play outside. So she drew this to pass the time."

"Not bad for a kid."

Deanna squeezed his hand. "I imagine this must be an archaeologist's dream discovery."

"It is."

"I found what I was looking for, too."

"You did?"

"Yes. I mentioned it earlier, but you brushed it away as an insane remark. Matthew wrote down his name and the date—1690. This confirms my suspicions. I know what to do now."

"You're saying that you really believe that your brother signed this wall in 1690?"

"Yes. In his former life."

"His former life." Justin stared at her and absorbed her words. "So you really are convinced that your brother's the reincarnation of Matthieu Landry. But I don't get it. Why? Because Matthew looks like the sea captain in that portrait? That could be a fluke. Because they share a first name? I know you miss Matthew. Be reasonable," he pleaded.

"I don't know how much of his twenty-first-century life he remembered," she continued, ignoring his words. "If he recollected anything about the modern world, I rather suspect that he didn't want to return to it. But I can't just give up on my brother. Would you?

Would you give up on me if I went missing?" She gave him a pointed look.

He shook his head.

"Justin, Sarah told me that certain power spots in Nature can transport you to other dimensions—if you're open to them, that is. I'm quite sure this is one of those portals."

She touched the painting of the seal basking on the rock. This time, the mural moved slightly. A wave stirred inside the picture. Salt water sprayed onto their faces. A gust of wind blew sand up into Justin's eyes. He was blinded. Before he could stop her, Deanna had firmly placed both palms on the cave drawings.

"Step away! The picture's alive! The wall's beginning to crack!" Justin exclaimed as soon as he could see again. It was too late—she had already leaned with all her weight onto the rock surface. The mural shimmered with light. Deanna melded into the seal. And then she was gone.

Justin blinked. His girlfriend had vanished. The rock wall continued glowing. He stepped back. He would be trapped inside the caves for some time, he suspected. He had thought she was overcome by raw emotion and lacked reason. Now he knew he was wrong. The ancient mural in the Cacouna Caves *was* a power spot. Deanna, just like her brother, had disappeared from the twenty-first century.

# FOURTEEN: TRANSITIONS

Matt got a text message as the car rolled into the fire station parking lot. "I'm fine. Don't worry about me. Deanna's okay, too, but something weird happened to her: she put her hand on the mural and disappeared. Please don't contact the authorities."

"What a bizarre text," Matt exclaimed. "So what's he saying? Don't go for help? Leave him to starve and suffocate? And Deanna vanished? What's that supposed to mean? It doesn't exactly relieve concerns."

A second text came in a few moments later. "I've got enough air, water, and energy bars to last for at least two days. Conserving iPhone battery. Need it for reading Wasaweg's manuscript. Ask Pierre to help you. He'll know how to get me out. Deanna will return. Don't worry."

Sarah repeated "Need it for reading" and burst out laughing. Then she started to cry. She blurted, "She got transported to another time. That's what happened in the cave, Matt. It *is* a power spot, I could feel it."

"I should've said no to this dumb-ass idea of hers." He gripped the steering wheel and looked straight ahead. "It's my fault; I drove us to the island. Now Justin's stranded and she's gone."

"Not your fault," Sarah placed a gentle hand on his shoulder. "She would've searched for the caves on her own, whether or not we'd gone with her. Something good has to come out of all this."

"Hope so," he grunted. "It's a race against time." He turned the key in the ignition and put the car into reverse, then the car screeched onto the road and barreled toward the cottage.

A dull blur of houses and farms whirred past. Matt felt numb. A sole pounding intent infused every cell in his body—*must rescue Justin, get him out before he suffocates. Then, try and pull Deanna back from wherever or whenever she has time travelled to. What a mess. Her poor parents. First one kid, and now the other, goes missing.*

For a long time, Matt and Sarah sat by the fireplace in the cottage and stared at the burning logs. Finally Sarah broke the silence. "Justin's an adult. He's been in high risk situations before. And he wrote that he was fine. We can't do anything tonight. You can stay over—there's a pullout sofa next to the fireplace in the living room. Let's return to the island in daylight. Tomorrow's Canada Day—no one will be at the dig. But I wish he hadn't said we shouldn't contact the authorities. It doesn't seem right."

"I still can't wrap my head around it. The whole story boggles my mind. Matthieu Landry, the sea captain who happens to be our common distant ancestor, sails to New France over three centuries ago. Lives there seven years and suddenly disappears. Some believe he drowns trying to cross from Cacouna Island to the mainland, but nobody actually finds his body. Then, a year ago, Matthew Aynsworth, Deanna's brother, fixates on a painting of Matthieu Landry, to whom he happens to look identical. He, too, vanishes without a trace; no one finds *his* body. Am I on the right track?"

"Yup, but you'll go nuts trying to figure it all out. I think Deanna connected some of the dots before we did. She concluded that Wasaweg's Matthieu was in fact her, Deanna's, Matthew. She realized her brother had drowned in the seventeenth century. So she decided to go back in time to try and stop it. It won't work, of course. You can't tamper with destiny." She sighed. "Her disappearance is the result of my blind-sightedness."

"Now it's *your* fault? How's that?"

"I'm the one who talked to her, again and again, about the power spots in Cacouna. I shouldn't have told her. I never knew she would find one. Those portals to other eras and dimensions—only a seasoned healer or visionary would know how to pass through them safely and reach the target destination. Deanna's wholly unprepared and untrained. Who knows *where* and *when* she ended up?"

"But they're just legends, Sarah."

"You *think?! Really?!*"

"You're right, you're right." He threw his hands up in the air. "And it's true; whatever I've thought of up to now to be 'real' went out the window a few hours ago, inside the caves. Look, we can try and rescue Justin, but Deanna, she's gone—to another dimension, as you said. And what can we do, Sarah, to change that? Nothing."

"Get some sleep, I guess, if possible. It might help us think more clearly in the morning. You can sleep on the pull-out sofa or, if you want more privacy, in the bedroom in the loft. God, life can be weird. Any time, it can throw something totally unexpected at you. I would never have thought that Justin and Deanna wouldn't be sleeping upstairs tonight."

"I know. I don't know what to think." Matt got up to give her a hug. The warm glow of the fire's embers cast a gold aura around their embrace—a light against the deep, surrounding darkness.

The next morning, as Matt crawled down the ladder from the loft, the smell of fresh coffee rose from the woodstove. Sarah was talking to Pierre in the kitchen. She shifted uncomfortably on her feet when Matt entered. He stood in the doorframe and glanced at the kitchen. The room seemed unusually untidy. Dishes piled up in the sink. Everything was in disarray. The laptop was, for once, closed on Sarah's corner table.

"I hope you don't mind. I told Pierre everything. He's trustworthy. Justin told us to contact him."

"A special power drill could break up the boulder that's trapping Justin," Pierre blurted.

"Fantastic!" Matt's careworn face creased into a smile.

"Yah, Pierre phoned the Rivière-du-Loup hardware store. Unfortunately, the drill's not in stock."

"I'd drive up to Quebec City and get it," Pierre said, "but it's only available in the Montreal outlet. It'll be delivered here within twenty-four hours. I told them I needed it ASAP."

"Good man!" Matt gave him an affectionate whack on the back.

"Can you guys get me up to speed on what's been happening? I'd like to go over the timeline of Deanna's recent activity before she vanished. I haven't spent much time with her, you know, since the day we walked to the Wolastoqiyik Wahsipekuk First Nation Centre. She texted me that she couldn't put down that manuscript you'd loaned us, Wasaweg's diary."

"She was *obsessed*," Matt said.

"I think she could relate to Wasaweg," said Sarah. "They both lost someone they loved. Neither of them ever got closure. That's what happens when someone goes missing."

"Yes, I saw that the day we first met," said Matt. "Apparently, I resemble her brother. She actually passed out! Did she tell you?"

Sarah nodded.

Matt continued, "It was clear to me that she's not over it."

"You never get over a loss like hers. You're lucky if you get through it," said Sarah.

"She showed me a photo," said Pierre. "Matt, you're the spitting image of Matthew Aynsworth. If I didn't know better, I'd think you were twins."

"You wanted to know about her recent activities?" said Sarah. "Well, first Deanna had that weird dream of a talking seal. After that, she kept taking off for the beach by herself. What else? She was fascinated by my ancestor's weaving and went into the barn several times a day to study it. And, oh!" She put her hand over her mouth.

"You're all over the place, but go on."

"It's likely nothing."

"No, every detail you remember is important," said Pierre.

"Okay. One more thing. She said that her brother would have left her a sign inside the Cacouna caves. She believed it would help her locate him. She kept shining her torch inside the caves, searching for his message. I found it baffling and disconcerting to see her so desperate and hopeful at the same time. After that, things happened way fast. A boulder crashed down from the ceiling. Luckily it didn't hit anyone. But it trapped Justin and Deanna inside the second cave. I don't remember much else. Thank God Justin's alive. I sure hope Deanna is, but we have no proof."

# FIFTEEN: DIANE

*The Island of Kakoua-Nak, 1687*

Deanna travelled through the dreamlands and passed into a black vortex of Time. She could almost taste the darkness as the stars' songs surrounded her. Then she plummeted through layers and layers of deep blue, purple, and mauve ether and landed on sand. When she opened her eyes, she was lying on a beach bordered by birch trees and strewn with green and brown algae. The sun was rising. A pale half moon hovered—barely visible—over the dark green line of the spruce trees on the hill. She savoured the rich smell of the forest and seaweed while trailing her fingers through fine, reddish sand grains. She felt inexplicably content. Then she noticed, at the edge of the woods a few metres away, a young man sitting watching her. Tall, slim, he wore clothes unlike anything she had ever seen. His black hair fell past his shoulders. His eyes and features were unmistakably recognizable. The man was her brother.

  She burst into tears of relief and joy and was starting to get up to run to him when he called out, "Mademoiselle, you have a small cut on your forehead." He moved toward her. "Did you hurt yourself on the rocks? It's easy enough to slip on the seaweed. Are you all right?"

  She nodded, unable to speak.

  "Who are you?" he asked.

  She found her voice at last. "It's Deanna! Don't you recognize me, Matthew?"

"You look familiar. But tell me, Diane, how do you know my name? Where are you from?" She gave him a bewildered look. When she didn't answer, he pointed to his canoe. "I was about to cross over to the mainland by canoe this morning and noticed you sleeping on the beach. I didn't want to disturb you, you slept so soundly, but I also didn't want to leave you alone, unprotected. I've been waiting for over an hour for you to wake up. Shall I take you back to the mainland?"

"No! Please don't make me leave!" Her spirits sank. How could he not know her? Why hadn't he rushed over to hug her? Did he have amnesia? Her own memory of recent events seemed pretty foggy. She had no idea how she had ended up on a beach on the island.

"Has someone mistreated you?" he asked. "Please don't cry. My wife will care for you. Come, follow me. I'll take you back to our home. You'd get lost in these woods without a guide."

Matthew married? Had he secretly eloped? Was that why he had run off? But that was unlike her brother; he surely would have brought his wife home to meet the family. Something was not right. Everything about him was the same and everything seemed skewed, different. She sprang to her feet and pointed toward the nearby mainland, the South Shore. "Hey! Where's the road that bridges the island to the mainland? Why are we surrounded by water? I don't see any people. Where is everyone?" She spluttered her questions in one breath.

"No road lies between Kakoua-Nak Island and the mainland. We cross over by canoe. It's the only way to leave the island, unless you're a good swimmer. I'm not." He stood up and began to walk away, indicating for her to follow.

She brushed the sand off her clothes and ran to catch up. They barely spoke as they walked. Matthew had always been a back-to-nature person, but this was ridiculous. Had some woman lured him to join a secret hippy commune on Cacouna Island or was he part of a strange cult? Was this why he hadn't contacted his family? And why was Cacouna Island suddenly not connected to the mainland at all? Did the earthquake cause major damage to the island and wash out the road that Matt had driven them over last night? She gulped as last night's events flooded back. Justin. Trapped in the middle cave. And she, somehow, had gotten out. All she remembered was pressing against the mural and everything going black.

At last they reached a path that climbed up a steep slope. Matthew pointed above and said, "We live at the top of the cliff. Live with us on Kakoua-Nak Island for as long as you please. The people on this island accepted me into their community when God saved me from the river's icy waters. They'll welcome you, too, since you come in peace and need our help."

When they reached the top of the cliff path, Deanna glimpsed a cluster of birch-bark-covered dwellings in the distance. A baby's wail pierced the stillness. They walked toward the clearing. A woman came out of a wigwam. She cradled an infant in her arms. A little girl stood shyly behind her with a small black cat at her side. The woman wore a red robe that covered the upper part of her body down to her knees—

as did her black hair. Her dress was decorated in yellow ochre geometric designs and dyed porcupine quills. Woven into her long hair were blue, star-shaped beaded flowers and half a dozen white feathers. She was barefoot.

"Papa! You returned!" the child darted out from behind her mother.

"Isabelle!" The man raced toward her and scooped her up in his arms.

The beautiful woman stepped forward and kissed the man. "Matthieu, you turned back? Is everything all right?"

"Yes, Wasaweg. I found this woman stranded on the beach."

Deanna stopped dead in her tracks. She knew without a doubt that she was face to face with the very woman whose story she had been reading for the past many days, the woman who had called Deanna's brother out of his life in the twenty-first century to live with her in seventeenth-century New France.

Within a few hours, Matthieu and Wasaweg had built a wigwam for Diane close to their own. Matthieu handed her some of his wife's clothing and several blankets. "You'll meet Émilie soon enough," he said. "She's from France. I noticed you're fluent in French, even though you're clearly English. Most foreigners in New France have no idea how to converse with the indigenous people. I learned tolerance from Wasaweg's family; they befriend all people, whatever their origins and language, as long as they come in peace, which I can see you do."

Deanna was about to blurt, *Of course I'm bilingual! Our parents enrolled us in the French immersion program at school. You pretty much have to be fluent in French to live as an Anglophone in Quebec.* Instead, she kept her words in check and asked, "Who is Émilie?"

"She arrived from France a few months before me. I met her at the monastery over on the mainland when I first landed in Kakona. Hers is a long, complicated story. She can tell you herself. I helped her out by adopting her cat, because the Mother Superior at her convent was going to take it away."

"That cute black cat in Isabelle's lap?"

He shook his head. "Nope. That's one of Bellevue's great-grandkittens. Turns out the cat was pregnant when I brought her over in the canoe with me. The great-grandmother cat is over in the woods now, probably hunting. Kakoua-Nak Island now has a small but growing cat population." He grinned.

Matthew had always loved cats. She remembered fighting with him when they were kids about who was going to get to sleep with their newly adopted cat Ludwiga. But if Bellevue the cat had already had kittens and those kittens had given birth, as well, it meant that Matthew had been on the island for even more than a year. *That doesn't make sense,* she thought. *He went missing twelve months ago.*

"You said that you met Émilie at the monastery on the mainland. Is it near the village?"

"The village?" Matthew looked puzzled. "Really, it's hardly a village—just a few settlers' homes and fishermen's cabins. The Jesuits live in a simple house by the beach right by the cove. There's a freshwater stream there, you see, and ships dock there to load barrels of salted produce from locals to bring back to France. The crews take the opportunity to renew their supply of fresh drinking water."

She was about to say, *They don't just go to the store to buy bottled water?* but checked herself in time.

"Also," her brother continued. "The settlers use the natural cove to come ashore. They unload their furniture and effects needed to settle close by."

Deanna flashed back to something she had read in a book about the history of Cacouna. "The trail that the shipmen and first settlers used to fetch fresh water later became, during the eighteenth century, a common road, now Rue du Quai." *So this is where Cacouna village begins,* she thought.

An awkward silence elapsed. Finally, Deanna broke it. "If it's all right with you, I think I'll retire for a few hours," she said. "My headache's worse. Thank Wasaweg for me for the loan of her clothes. I'm most grateful you're letting me stay with you guys until I recover from my head injury. I don't imagine I'll stay long, but thank you."

Just then a young European woman, around twenty, burst into the clearing, surrounded by a group of laughing Mi'gmaq children. She wore a big smile and her blue eyes were sparkling beneath her sopping brown hair. "We went for a dip in the river, Matthieu, despite the cold! Lentug dared me to, and I did it!" She stopped in her tracks as she saw Deanna. "Who's this?" she asked. Then she collected her manners and made a small curtsey. "*Excusez-moi.*" (Excuse me.) "How impolite. I'm Émilie. What's your name?"

"She's Diane," introduced Matthew.

Before Deanna could interject that her name was not Diane, Émilie had rushed over and given her a big hug.

"Wonderful! You're so pretty! You have a perfect nose! I'm envious. You look English. Are you?"

Deanna nodded.

The girl continued: "Do you think you could teach me some English? I'm learning Mi'gmaq," she looked down modestly. Then, her innate vivaciousness and confidence overruled any false humility. "I want to master all three languages. This country is so wonderful—it gives us many diverse opportunities. Of course, my faith in human beings was restored only because these kind people adopted me into their family. I escaped the convent and ran away to the island a few months after Matthieu adopted my cat." She took a breath. "Have you met Bellevue?" She rattled on. "You know I hated this place when I first arrived here from France. It's *so* cold in the winter that even the salty river freezes over! Can you imagine? And did you know that they wanted me to marry an ugly old man who was four times my age? The only way to get out of it was to try to become a nun, but that was pretty bad, too. I love God, but my God, the way they bossed me around at the convent, all in the name of the Lord, it was horrible! I'm sure Jesus Christ would feel so sorry about what some people are doing down here in His Name!"

Émilie was a chatterbox, no doubt, but she was full of joie de vivre. Deanna burst out laughing. She looked forward to hearing the girl's stories and decided to start taking notes on everything she was learning about this time period. From the way Matthew had been talking, it sounded like he had arrived in New France quite a bit earlier. She asked him, "Would you mind telling me the date today?"

"June twenty-third," he replied.

"No, I mean the year. I think you're right that I hit my head on a rock. My memory's pretty fuzzy."

"1687," Matthieu and Émilie blurted at the same time. They glanced at each other and laughed.

"1687," Deanna repeated aloud, to herself as much as to them. She thought, *Uh oh. I have travelled way too far back in time. I'm three years away from the 1690 English invasion of the island. I guess I had better get used to being here.*

She took in her surroundings. A hawk swooped past and alighted on a tall spruce next to her new home. She smelled burning logs and looked around to see the source. Wasaweg waved at her cheerfully from a distance. She was stoking a campfire.

"We'll eat together after sundown. I hope you're hungry, Diane. I'm preparing a welcome feast."

Deanna waved back. *I could get used to this,* she thought. *Anyway, no turning back now.*

That night, she lay down on the floor of her wigwam and stared at the bright stars through the opening at the top. She thought about how Matthew had adopted all the Mi'gmaq ways and customs. Even his features and expressions resembled those of the island's inhabitants. Had she not known otherwise, she would have thought he was First Nations from birth. She wondered how she herself would transform in the next three years. She started counting the stars. Soon she drifted into sleep.

# SIXTEEN: DELIVERANCE

*The Cacouna Caves, Twenty-first Century*

"Stand back," Pierre said. Sarah and Matt stayed outside the entrance to the caves and peered in at him. He plunged the power drill into the boulder that blocked off the entrance to the second cave. The drill-bit sank in and then an earth-shattering noise blasted as the rock exploded and blue sparks flew everywhere. The huge boulder cracked in half like a giant grey egg. When the rocks stopped rattling, Pierre motioned to the others to stay where they were and squeezed his lean body through the narrow opening in the rock. "No one here!" he shouted. "But an LED light is flashing further in. Justin must have gone into the third cave. Hang on."

Ten minutes later, they heard shuffling movements.

"I need a hand!" Pierre yelled from inside the second cave. They rushed to help him. "Take him," he said. He held Justin's limp body in his arms and maneuvered it so he could slide it sideways through the narrow opening.

"Is he alive?" Matt asked as he received the body.

"His lips are blue and his breathing's shallow. He needs oxygen."

"We'll drive directly to the Rivière-du-Loup hospital. No point waiting for an ambulance."

"No. No hospitals." Justin gasped out the words and struggled in Matt's arms. "What do you think I am? A wimp? Put me down. I need fresh air that's all. No better place than next to the Saint Lawrence River."

Justin sat propped up against a rock while the others gathered in a semicircle around him. The tide was way out and the sand was damp from the earlier high tide. A long, thick line of brown seaweed marked the point to which the water had risen in the morning. Sarah spread a blanket and put out a thermos of coffee. She poured some coffee for Justin.

"First hot drink in more than twenty-four hours. Thanks for bringing the thermos, Sarah. What took you guys so long to get here?"

"I told Pierre what happened to you," Sarah said. "He came up with a plan of action right away, but we had to wait for the power drill to arrive from Montreal. You texted us not to contact anyone else. The local firefighters could have helped quicker."

"I'm glad you got my two texts. After I sent them, I lost the signal. I didn't want the authorities involved because it would have gotten you in trouble. Also, I figured Pierre would know how to break up big boulders because of his job as a landscaper. You got my second text about Deanna vanishing, right?"

Until then, no one had mentioned her name. "Yes," said Sarah. "While we waited for the drill to arrive, we talked a ton about her. It's pretty clear that she time travelled from the cave. That's why she's gone. She's alive, but God knows where and when she landed. What can we do to get her back, Justin?"

"I may have figured out where she went. The two books I had in my knapsack gave me a lot of food for thought and some insights. I'm pretty sure I'd have gone nuts in the caves without them. They took my mind off my situation." He glanced at Matt. "You handed Wasaweg's diary to me minutes before the earthquake. I also had the book that Pierre had bought in the antique shop." He directed his next words to Pierre. "Can I mention that *Cacouna's History* is a mind-numbingly boring book because of the way it's written? Whatever made you decide to spend fifty dollars on it?"

"Actually, Deanna purchased it for me. Real generous of her as it was so pricey. I wanted to read it as research for the website I'm building. But then I got too busy landscaping, so I loaned it to her."

"She told me she tried reading it, but got disinterested." Sarah piped up.

"Well, she passed Scott's book on to me, and so it was in my backpack, too. I'm not surprised she got turned off by its crusty, antiquated language; still, the content was interesting. To research her book, the author studied fur traders' journal entries and letters to their families about life in New France. I was struck by a description, from one man's diary, of an unnamed white woman who lived on Cacouna Island. She never visited the other foreigners living at the trading posts along the Saint Lawrence River, never left the island until the English invasion—after which she vanished without a trace. Here, I bookmarked the passage." He pulled the volume from his knapsack.

*We were canoeing near Cacouna Island and stopped for fresh water. We caught a rare glimpse of the foreign woman who lived with the French man's family and whom everyone talked about on the mainland, but whom no one had ever met. We watched her and two small children sitting on a log by the campfire. She spoke French fluently with them, but we heard her teaching them to read in English. She didn't talk the way New Englanders do. We couldn't identify her accent. In fact, we could barely discern if she were a real person or a sprite hovering in the light-dappled forest. She had deep blue, melancholic, far-away eyes. Her hair was long and black and she wore it in the style of the Mi'gmaq—in two braids. She was exquisite. I'll never forget her. People say she lived on the island for three years and that after the English invasion no one ever saw her again. It was as if she had never been ...*

"After I read this passage I felt hope again," said Justin. "I had seen Deanna press both palms against the mural. In the blink of an eye, she had disappeared. I now believe she travelled back to the time in which Wasaweg and Matthieu were raising their children on Cacouna Island."

"I agree. It would make total sense," Sarah interjected. "She was so stressed about the loss of her brother. I think that once she read Wasaweg's diary, Deanna connected most of the dots in the mystery about why he had gone missing. She figured out that Matthew was, in another lifetime, Matthieu Landry. That's why she deliberately leaned into the mural and hoped it would be the portal to the era he had returned to."

"So when Deanna got sucked through the mural, she reappeared in New France," Justin said. "She is the woman whom the fur traders described in their letters and journals: the foreign woman who lived for years with the French man's family on Cacouna Island."

"Years?" Pierre blurted. "She's been gone two days!"

"I guess you weren't paying attention, Pierre, when I read the passage. *'People say she lived on the island for three years.'* It's not impossible to believe, providing you accept that that's how time travel works." Justin explained. "It's like the famous phrase Samuel Coleridge coined. I remember Deanna, who had to study it in her English lit class, reading it to me: 'Imagination is the willing suspension of disbelief.' So let's say you willingly suspend your disbelief and, rather, imagine that you're now on a spacecraft hurtling toward Mars. Over many, many months, you traverse hundreds of thousands of kilometres. When you return to Earth, not that much time will have passed in earthly time, but your bones will be brittle because of osteoporosis as if you're an extremely old person. I imagine time travel is a lot like space travel, only your body wouldn't, hopefully, be adversely affected when you returned to Earth. I bet your mind is never the same, though." He kept his worst fears to himself. *But if Matthew and Deanna ever make it back to our millennium, who knows if they can ever acclimatize to the modern world ... especially Matthew. She's been gone a couple of days, but he's been missing for more than a year in modern time. Who knows how many years that translates into of his journey back in time?*

Matt had been observing everyone speak and had remained silent until now. "I don't get it. What did she hope to accomplish?" he asked. "Assuming your theories are legit and Matthieu Landry *is* Matthew Aynsworth, did Deanna really think she could convince him to return to the twenty-first century?"

"Maybe," said Sarah. "Or maybe all this was way beyond control—the force of her attachment to her brother simply pulled her back in time, like metal to a magnet."

"I think it's selfish," Matt said. "What about Wasaweg? Deanna wants him back here in this time, but Matthieu Landry was a man who was happily married to Wasaweg in that other era. Did Deanna ever consider how Matthieu's wife would feel once he was gone?"

"Matt, you haven't read the full diary," interjected Pierre. "You told me yourself that day we met up at the First Nation Centre—when you offered to loan it to us. I think you said it was too tragic so you didn't want to read it. My point is that Wasaweg would have to live out her life as a widow. That's indisputable. But Matthew, he's a young man. Just twenty. With his life ahead of him. Wouldn't it be wonderful if Deanna could succeed in getting him back to live with his parents, his sister, and all his friends? And you, you'd get to meet him—your doppelganger."

Matt shook his head. "I was into going to the caves because of the drawings. But I would never have supported this crazy idea of Deanna's about travelling back in time and trying to steal Matthieu Landry from his life with the Mi'gmaq. Typical English," he muttered under his breath to Sarah. "And no. I wouldn't want to meet him no matter how much he looks like me. So what? Let him live and die in Wasaweg's time. That's where he was meant to be. You see him as Matthew Aynsworth, an English man gone missing from his home in Upper Westmount, hoity-toity English land. I see him as Matthieu Landry, my ancestor's husband, the source of so many of my relatives in Cacouna. Let Deanna stay there with him if she's so attached." He got up and walked to the water's edge, hands in his pocket, out of earshot.

"I'm so sorry, Justin. He doesn't know what he's saying," Sarah said. "He's been beside himself since the earthquake. He keeps trying to be strong, and then he loses it. I've never seen him like this. Neither of us has slept in about forty-eight hours, though that's no excuse for his insensitivity. Please forgive him."

"He's acting real strange," Justin admitted. "What is it, ever since we got on the island, people are not themselves?"

Sarah refilled his cup and tipped out the last dregs of coffee from the thermos. She put on a cheerful smile. "Well I'm happy, at least happier than this morning when I woke up. I think we should go back to the cottage and celebrate that we got you out."

"Definitely!" Pierre said. He picked up Justin's knapsack and helped him up. "But still, whatever our ideas about why and where Deanna time travelled, the fact remains that even though you're free, your girlfriend is missing and so is her brother. We still have no idea about how to get them back."

"Killjoys, all of you men!" Sarah glared at him. She turned to Justin: "What if we re-enter the caves? You said that when Deanna placed her hands on the ancient mural, she passed through it. I'm willing to go back in and try."

"Thanks. It's no good. I already tried. Wall's totally cracked now," Justin said tersely. He stood up. "Let's drive to the cottage." They started walking back in the direction of the car.

Sarah and Matt walked ahead hand in hand. Justin, meanwhile, leaned on Pierre and moved slowly and dejectedly. He felt like an old man whose sole flickering hope had been extinguished even before it had had a chance to shine.

A woman's yell broke the silence. It came from the caves.

# SEVENTEEN: THE FORMIDABLE PROFESSOR

"Hey you!" the woman shouted. Everyone had turned around.

An attractive but imposing woman in her early thirties stood in front of the cave entrance. Matt and Sarah backtracked quickly toward her, scrambling over the rocks and boulders. Justin hung back. He still felt weak, and, to his horror, he had recognized his project supervisor.

As they approached her, they saw the woman raise her cell phone in one hand and wave it midair like a weapon. "I'm calling the police! You're trespassing! Guilty of criminal activity!" Her shrill, angry voice pierced the air.

Sarah pulled herself up onto a big rock and faced her. "My friend back there—" she pointed at Justin "is unwell. We came because we heard you scream and thought you needed our help."

"I know who your friend is and what you've done—broken the lock on the gate and trespassed! That's a chargeable offence. I'll make sure you're prosecuted—each and every one of you. I've just looked at the caves and seen rocks strewn everywhere. Thanks to your recklessness, those priceless cave drawings are likely irreparably damaged."

"Use your iPhone," Sarah retorted. "Look up recent earthquakes and seismic activity in Quebec. Less than forty-eight hours ago, a minor earthquake struck—

the epicentre was right here—only metres from where you're standing. You'll see it registered 4.6 on the Richter scale. Justin and his girlfriend got trapped inside. You could show some compassion."

"His girlfriend? I only see one woman—you. Where did she go?"

Sarah didn't answer.

"I think you're hiding something from me." She smirked. "Tell me *why* you were inside the caves in the first place." The woman's lips curled down. "Justin has disobeyed my orders. I am Professor Jones, his supervisor. You'd better tell your friend he's not only off the team, I'll report him to the university, too, and make sure he never gets a decent job again. He'll be washing dishes for the rest of his life."

"What's so bad about washing dishes?" Sarah burst out. This seemed to inflame the woman's rage. Her smirk changed to an angry glare. "I do it three times a day at the B&B my mom and I run. It's a mindless, de-stressing activity. You should try it. Might get you to lighten up and relax a bit."

Pierre had caught up by now and whispered to Sarah. "Not helping! Let me have a go at chilling her out. We don't want criminal charges thrown at us." He inched closer to Professor Jones. As he drew near, he couldn't help but notice that she was about five years older than himself. She wore an olive-coloured mini jumpsuit that brought attention to her green eyes and long legs and curvy figure. Her perfume was alluring.

"Looks like he's trying to lure a gorgeous wild animal from its lair." Justin muttered. He had managed to climb the rocks and rejoin his companions. "It's

Shakespeare's 'Taming of the Shrew' all over again. What a shrill voice she has! It could break glass."

"We *could* try and give her the benefit of the doubt," Sarah reasoned, forgetting to whisper. "Maybe she *is* just a dedicated—albeit bitter—academic who wants to make sure that the cave drawings are kept in pristine condition."

"You know I can hear you." Professor Jones glared. She waved her iPhone at Sarah and opened her mouth to say something snippy, but got thrown off balance. Her right heel caught on a loose stone outside the cave's entrance. She toppled over and fell backwards, narrowly missing the iron gate. She cried out in pain and grasped her ankle.

Pierre raced to her side and helped her to her feet. "Are you okay?"

"My ankle! It's sprained." She groaned.

"Here. Don't put any weight on it. Wrap your hands around my neck." He leaned over. "One, two, three." He lifted her and held her in his arms. "Now you're good. Don't worry, we'll get you home."

"Thank you." Her eyes teared up.

Pierre smiled down at her. "It's the eve of Canada Day. What are you doing out here anyway? You shouldn't be working on a holiday. You're extremely dedicated to your job." He gave her an admiring look. "We can drive you to your lodgings in the village, but I have a suggestion: why not return with us to Sarah's cottage over toward L'Anse au Persil and join us for a late dinner? I've pre-cooked a delicious meal and the food is waiting to be eaten. We'll talk things over with a good bottle of Chardonnay. I'll ice your ankle. I'm a landscaper, so I'm always straining my muscles. I'm happy to massage some cream on your foot if it's not too tender. I'll personally drive you back to your room after dinner. What do you say?"

Sarah rolled her eyes and Justin looked aghast at Pierre's outrageous flirtation with the professor. It was working: her chiselled features seemed to melt and her mouth creased into a smile which made her appear beautiful.

"That's sweet. Call me Angela. What's your name?"

Back at the guesthouse after dinner, Justin slowly climbed the ladder to the loft. He lit a scented candle and placed it on the bedside table next to the queen-sized bed. The low murmur of blended voices rising up from the living room below was especially comforting after his long hours spent alone in the dark caves. Even the drone of Angela's voice, which, up until now, had chilled him to the bone, sounded warm and pleasant, even melodic. The wine and Pierre's charm seemed to be working its magic on her. Under drooping eyelids, he watched the shadows dance on the sloped ceiling of the candlelit loft. He drifted toward sleep and instinctively reached for Deanna. Her side of the bed was cold. The oncoming tide of sleep reversed in that instant and he remembered all that had transpired. She, too, was in the lower Saint Lawrence region, but she was resting—more than three centuries behind them—in a wigwam somewhere on Cacouna Island.

# EIGHTEEN: DISCLOSURE

*New France, 1690*

Deanna heard the sound of something rummaging in the bracken outside her wigwam. *Was it a porcupine?* She hoped it wasn't a foraging bear. A small, chubby fist pushed the flap aside and Isabelle's smiling face appeared. "Diane, can I sleep in your wigwam tonight? Mama said it's OK. Matthis has a toothache. She and Émilie are taking turns looking after him."

"Sure, Izzy."

The six-year-old girl ducked in. How she had grown in the three years that Deanna had spent living on the island. The child wore her hair in two long braids and shared her mother's features. She had Matthieu's wide, smiling mouth.

"Tell me the story again of why you write those funny squiggly marks on the birch bark wall hanging above your head? How many lines are there now?" The little girl pointed to rows and rows of centimetre-long charcoal lines scratched onto a gigantic piece of birch bark that Diane had hung over her bed.

"At least a thousand lines, Isabelle. You know why. We go over this every time you have a sleepover. At the end of the day, I make a line to mark each and every day that I've been blessed to live with you and your family." She gave her a quick hug. She never revealed her real reason. She felt so privileged to live within Wasaweg and Lentug's community, but her appreciation for their ways and culture could not—nor would she let it—completely erase the memory of her life with Matthew and her parents in Montreal. She missed Justin and constantly worried about whether or not they had rescued him from the middle cave. Nor could her deep attachment to Wasaweg's family override her underlying dejection; she had had to quietly accept that her brother had absolutely no inkling that she was his sister from Montreal. To live with someone you loved and be reminded at every moment that they did not feel the same familial connection was gut wrenching. The dismal truth was that she had arrived on the island three full years before Wasaweg's family's departure for the mainland. She had learned the hard way that time travel, like life, was totally unpredictable. It had happened (perhaps as a fluke) that she had been in the right spot (the Cacouna caves) at the right time (when the earthquake struck and stirred up potent magic dormant in the mural), but had travelled to the wrong time. It was like when she was sixteen and her mother had planned a whole trip around celebrating the New Year in Australia, but had miscalculated the difference in time. Their family had arrived in Sydney a day early. In that instance, it was a simple miscalculation of the time zones and they had only had to wait a few hours before they could check into their hotel and watch the fireworks over the Sydney Harbour. But now she had been forced to wait until 1690 to see whether or not destiny could be changed. She had grown thin worrying about her parents. She hoped that time passed differently for them. Otherwise, who knew if they'd still be alive when or if she returned to Montreal? How naïve to think that she could arrive on the island in the nick of time to save her brother from drowning. Instead, she was being forced to spend three years away from her family and Justin until that fateful point in time would arrive. Her father's words haunted her: "You're rushing into it. You always do this, Deanna." She had once again acted impulsively, gone with her heart, and not thought about the repercussions of her actions. How stupid! She had no guarantee that she could even get Matthew and herself back to the future. Her parents might end up losing both kids. It would break their hearts. She grew increasingly pessimistic about the outcome of her mission, more so as she witnessed Matthew grow in his love for his wife and kids. How could she rip him out of his blissful life? He had never looked this happy in modern times.

Roughly one thousand and thirty days and nights had passed. Only thirty more to go until the English would invade the island. This she knew from the timeline of events described in Wasaweg's diary. Soon, in late autumn, the family would flee to the ancient caves. From the cove on the north-western tip of Cacouna Island, they would canoe across the water to make a new life on the plot next to Bernard Beaumont's land. Matthieu Landry would not make it to the mainland.

The little girl pinched her arm. "Diane! Have you seen a ghost? You got all pale and have been staring into space for the past five minutes. Where did you go? You haven't heard a word I've spoken!"

"I'm sorry. What were you saying?"

The little girl jumped into her arms and pointed at the right-hand bottom corner of the birch bark wall hanging. "I want to know what this new thing is that you scribbled over here? 'Deanna and Justin.'" She gave her a keen look. "Are *you* Deanna? Then why does Papa call you Diane? I'd hate it if people called me by the wrong name!"

Isabelle was quite the chatterbox, rather like Émilie. She was also astute.

"You're right. I should have told your dad right from the beginning that my name is not Diane but Deanna. He misheard. But it's just a name. Who cares? It won't make a difference." She sighed. Matthew lacked the capacity to recall his future; hence, he didn't know her. She should coin a term to describe his condition, one which was the very opposite of amnesia. He wasn't forgetful of his past. What Matthew was experiencing was the utter eradication of all memory of both his future incarnation and the very moment when he had sprung back from it to return to his past life. She understood—but most people would not be able to grasp—the concept of reincarnation. It explained, albeit in mystic terms, the continuity of the soul's existence. Bodies died, souls did not.

"So who is Justin? Is he your husband? Do you miss him? I know Mama misses Papa whenever he goes exploring with Uncle Lentug up and down the South Shore. She cries at night. I pretend I don't hear, but she sniffles."

"No, Izzy. Justin's not my husband. I had hoped he *might* become my husband in future, but then we got separated suddenly. And yes, I miss him every waking moment."

"Is that why you never talk about him? How did you two get separated?"

"It's way too complicated to explain."

"What does 'complicated' mean? Did he die?"

Children were so open and to the point—not shy to ask the meaningful questions in life. "No, sweetie." Deanna hugged Isabelle. *Justin didn't die. Justin isn't even born, but I can't tell her that, can I?* "He hasn't died. He'll be waiting for me, so I don't want to forget him—not even for a day."

"Did you and Justin kiss when you were together?" She gave a mischievous wink that belied her age.

"It's a secret. Now go to sleep."

She left Isabelle tucked under her wool blanket. The child's breathing grew more and more slow and even. Deanna crawled out of the wigwam, stood up, and stretched.

"Over here!" Émilie whispered. "I couldn't sleep either. Maybe it's the full moon. Want to sit with me?"

They sat shoulder to shoulder on the log by the campfire. "Must be close to midnight."

"Dunno. I lose track of time on the island. Do you find that, too, Diane?"

She shook her head.

"It was totally different at the convent. I'm used to waking up before dawn, because my parents owned a big farm in north-western France and I helped Papa milk the cows and feed the horses. But at the convent, we always had to rush to attend matins, communion, and vespers. Everything was regimented."

"Kind of like school, eh?"

"I didn't go to school. My younger brother got the chance." She stared at the ground.

"Your writing has improved by leaps and bounds." Deanna had begun teaching English to Wasaweg's family and Émilie soon after she had arrived on the island. Three years later, they were all fluent and literate, except for Matthis, of course, who was still too young to read or write, yet had started speaking three languages.

"Thank you." Émilie reached out and took her hand. "If my parents could see me now, they'd be proud. I miss them, my three sisters, and two brothers. Do you have siblings? You never talk about your family. It's weird."

"My parents must be desperately hoping for my return, but I know for a fact that my brother doesn't miss me in the least, which really hurts …" Her words trailed off and a long silence fell. Émilie was sensitive not to pry further. Deanna decided to open up a little to the young French woman. "I'd love to be cheerful like you. You're always smiling and laughing. I, on the other hand, tend to be melancholic. When I lived with my parents before I left my—my home, I was extremely unhappy. My brother, you see, had left us suddenly. Our family felt tremendous shock and uncertainty about his fate."

"Oh that's too bad! I'm sorry, Diane. Did he go to war? Was he a soldier? I'm sure you'll see him again."

Deanna shook her head. "No, he didn't. It's complicated." *What supreme irony. She has no idea that I see him daily and it only makes my heart heavier because he doesn't recognize me.* Her eyes welled up and stung from holding back the tears. She swallowed. "I'm grateful to have lived here with all of you. You've become my second family—but I miss my parents and homeland all the time. I'll leave you soon. I'm restless. The time to pick up and move is around the corner, I feel it coming. I'm never content, Émilie. I always miss someone or long for something. The mountains seem more beautiful when I see them from a distance. I want to cross to the other side of the river one day and see the North Shore, even though people have told me that when you reach it, the beautiful blueness that drew you over, is no longer blue when you get there." She thought of Sarah. It felt like only a few hours had passed since they'd stood on the porch outside the cottage and gazed at the mountains together. How she wished she could see Sarah again and enjoy a good cup of English tea. And yet, if she ever returned to the twenty-first century, she would miss Émilie, too, more so, she realized with a shock, because Émilie would long be dead." Her tears started trickling down.

"You can say more." The girl squeezed her hand. "I know this is simmering inside you. Don't get all quiet now."

"Well, what's the point of hoping for things not to change? They always do. Yet, I can't shake the wish for a happy ending. Actually," she blurted, "I hate missing people. I can't stand it. It weighs my heart down. Why can't all the people you've ever loved be with you in one place? When I was a child, I never wished for anything or felt I was missing out. Why can't

I be like that again?" The tears streamed down her cheeks.

"You're a romantic," Émilie said, and stroked her back. "You want heaven to come on earth. Personally, I never expect to be happy and I don't expect anyone to understand me—if it happens, it's Grace. Things change all the time. A bird could fly out of a wall—I wouldn't be surprised. I've seen the best of human nature and the worst of it. The Lord's presence is my solace." She put both arms around Deanna and hugged her tightly, talking all the while. "Jesus said: 'Become like a child to enter the kingdom of heaven.' I don't think he meant that heaven is a distant realm. It's in your heart and in every breath. It's your spirit and gives you life. It's what absorbs you in its infinite arms in the moment people mistakenly call death. Pouring your heart out like this is good; it means right now you're as open as a child. You don't have to be so grown up, Diane, and bear the burdens of the world."

"That's both wise and sweet." She disengaged herself from Émilie's embrace. "Your faith inspires me. You mean what you say. You know, I never like it," she confided, "when religious people parrot platitudes like 'You'll only be happy when you remember God.' It makes me feel as if a threat hangs over my head and I'll be punished if I don't follow their advice. To me, being spiritual is not the same as being religious. I'm spiritual. In my own way, I remember God. But I often doubt that God remembers me! That's my quandary!" She laughed at herself.

"Don't you think that when *you* remember God, God knows and feels it? It is He who is remembering

Himself in your thought. So you're always united! But I agree with you that religious groups too often hold out carrots and sticks as if we're all idiots! I don't believe that only priests and bishops know truth. We don't need an intermediary to be one with God. Fear only inspires more fear. Faith by affirmation of divine love is so sweet and soft, it sneakily creeps into your heart and waters it with love, lets you blossom. That's why I left the convent. I wanted freedom to worship God the way I wanted. I'd heard the Mi'gmaq had accepted Matthieu and made him feel at home. I figured if they welcomed one European, they'd welcome another. And the funny thing is—I've never felt like a refugee or a foreigner here."

\*\*\*

Justin looked out of the attic window and caught a glimpse of Professor Jones as she circled the barn. She was limping. She appeared to be searching for something.

"What's the prof still doing here?" he asked Sarah as soon as he entered the kitchen.

"You'd better get used to calling her Angela. She and Pierre hit it off. She slept over at his place, can you believe it? And she's been wandering, hobbling, all over the property ever since I woke up. It's pretty weird." She opened the small kitchen window and called out through the screen. "Angela, come join us for breakfast. Tell Pierre to bring a pot of his fabulous espresso. I'll provide the rest."

Within half an hour, everyone had gathered around the oak table in the living room.

"So this property once belonged to Bernard Beaumont?" Angela asked Sarah, as she buttered a croissant and piled a thick layer of blueberry jam on top of the butter.

"Yup. He and his wife Isabelle plowed the land and built the barn. Her uncle, Lentug, a First Nations healer, helped lay the foundations to the wooden structure they decided to erect in place of wigwams. Bernard later built extensions on the original cabin, *et voilà!* You see our rustic cottage!"

"That reminds me, Sarah," Justin said, "You told Deanna and me that Bernard's father, Charles de Beaumont, had stolen royal jewels belonging to the French King and that they were never recovered."

"That's right."

"Well, I found a clue in Wasaweg's diary about the whereabouts of the missing gems."

"Oh? I figured they hadn't survived the shipwreck." Strangely, Sarah didn't seem happy about the news. She lightly kicked at Justin under the table; instead, she got Matt who thought she was flirting. He leaned over and draped his arm around the back of her chair.

"Yes. The information's embedded in the glossary of Mi'gmaq terms at the end of Wasaweg's journal. If I hadn't been stuck in the cave and wanting to distract myself, I'd probably never have plowed through it and discovered the clues."

"Don't keep us hanging in suspense! Tell us where the damn Crown Jewels are!" said Pierre.

"Yes, Justin, do tell," Angela said, in a nonchalant voice, as if she could care less, but her green eyes sparkled with interest.

Justin realized he was trapped. He had no wish to disclose to Professor Jones, of all people, where the lost Crown Jewels had been hidden. She had blended in, like a duck sitting among a gaggle of Canada geese, and he had forgotten to be wary of her. Now he was in a bind, because he had announced he had news to share.

Angela grabbed the manuscript from his hands. "Fascinating! Let's have a look-see." She flipped to the back of the journal—where he'd inserted a bookmark. "Your throat's kind of raspy, Justin, likely from all those hours you spent in the cave. Why don't I read this aloud instead of you?" Before he could reclaim the book, she had started reading:

My son-in-law got a letter from his estranged father, Charles de Beaumont, who wished to reconcile. Bernard refused to reply. A few months later, de Beaumont died and his secretary, Philippe Dumont, knocked at our door. He had travelled all the way from de Beaumont's seigneurie to bequeath Bernard with a gift from his late father. "Your inheritance," the man said, and handed over a small package. "Your father deeply regretted disowning you. He left you this. He asked that you pray for his soul so that he could be redeemed of his grave misdeeds. Open the package after I leave and never tell a soul what's inside. It's yours to do with as you please." Philippe exited the cottage as quickly as he had entered it.

Bernard slid the unopened parcel into the back of the armoire next to the fireplace. Years passed. One rainy day, Isabelle discovered the package when she was clearing out the drawers. "Shall I throw this out or open it?" she asked. "I hope to God nothing perishable is inside, Bernard. It would be rotten. It's been sitting here for the last ten years."

"Have it your way, then," Bernard grunted. "Open it."

I'll never forget the moment my daughter sat in the rocking chair next to the fire and removed the yellowed wrapping paper. She gasped. "Mon Seigneur!"

We all rushed over. In Isabelle's lap lay three diamonds, a ruby the size of a thimble, and an emerald the size of my thumb.

Strangely, Bernard's eyes filled with tears. "Remove them," he blurted. "They have the stink of sin. I want no part of de Beaumont's legacy. He preferred to save these royal jewels from the sinking, shipwrecked ship rather than rescue a human being—your father. He persecuted Matthieu for the crime that he, Charles de Beaumont, had committed against the French King."

Isabelle nodded. "I understand why you don't want them. I don't, either. But what do we do now?"

"I don't want them in our cottage. They're cursed. Hide the gems inside the wall in the barn facing the river."

Just then, my youngest grandson missed the bottom rung of the ladder coming down from the loft and started bawling at the top of his lungs. Isabelle raced to tend to him.

"Would you deal with it, Wasaweg?" Bernard asked me. He bent over to stoke the fire—as if nothing had happened, as if the treasure did not exist.

I clenched the Crown Jewels in my hand and marched to the barn. Bernard's contempt for them was understandable. I, too, glanced at them with disdain. *These may be worth buckets of gold coins, but they are worthless, more useless than the dust on the windowsills. Of what value are they to a broken family? They cannot bring our Matthieu home.*

I hid the royal jewels inside the barn wall and nailed a board over the hole. We thought that if our children, or their children, were ever in need, they might discover the buried treasure. I'm leaving this record in my journal. If you're reading my words and you're my descendant, the gems are yours to do with as you see fit.

Angela closed the diary.

"Well, that's timely!" said Pierre. "We have Wasaweg's descendants gathered around your dining table, Sarah! Justin and I are the only ones here who don't have any claim."

"And the professor—you forgot to mention that she's got nothing to do with the jewels," Justin interjected. "Sarah and Matt are related to Wasaweg and Matthieu Landry and therefore entitled to the lost gems,"

"Actually ..." Pierre began.

"You're kidding." Justin stared at him. A terrible thought had begun to percolate in his mind.

Pierre squeezed Angela's hand across the dining table. "Jones isn't her maiden name, you know. She confided to me last night that she has been using her married name professionally. She's divorced, but she never reverted to her original surname."

She nodded meekly and stroked his hand with her long fingers. Justin thought her scarlet fingernails looked like fish hooks dripping with blood from a fresh catch.

"I'm sorry, babe. I know I promised I wouldn't say anything, but the picture's changed now." Pierre glanced at Angela. He directed his next words to Sarah, who sat across the table from him. "Angela's a Beaumont originally from Quebec City. A distant relative of yours who has been in search of the jewels. She kept your familial connection a secret, because disclosing it could hurt her career—it might look as if she had vested interests in working in the Cacouna region."

"You betcha," Justin muttered under his breath.

"But now that it's about to come out, you should accept her as family, no?" Pierre was clearly head over heels infatuated with his new lady.

"Impossible!" Sarah blurted. "All the women in the Beaumont family use their maiden name, even after marriage. It's a centuries-old family tradition."

"Unless they've got an ulterior motive," Justin growled. "Unless they're actually hunting for lost jewels that are hundreds of years old and millions of dollars in value. Am I right?" He glared at his supervisor.

"I'm a Beaumont through and through." Angela straightened her shoulders with great dignity. "I've sought the jewels for years. When I was a little girl, my granny told me the family secret—that on his deathbed, Charles de Beaumont bequeathed the jewels to his youngest son, Bernard, who lived near Cacouna. Grandmamma Beatrice told me all kinds of tales that she'd picked up from locals. She had heard about the

Cacouna Caves and that they hid great treasure. I put two and two together. I deciphered the mystery on my own," she said proudly, "and I decided to look for the jewels inside the caves. It was the reason I became an archaeologist—to get permission to explore the caves. Why else would I have come to Cacouna, this tiny, out-of-the-way rural community?"

"I don't get why you're gloating," retorted Sarah. "The only treasures in the caves are the ancient drawings; there never were any jewels there. You know absolutely nothing about my family history. Bernard Beaumont never entered the Cacouna Caves. He never even visited the island; rather, he picked Wasaweg up on the mainland the day she and her family fled the English who had attacked their home."

"Who cares about history? All I know is that I'm as entitled to the jewels as Matt and Sarah are, if not more. I'm descended from Joseph Beaumont, Charles de Beaumont's first-born son, a man who did not run away from home and was never disowned by his father." She inched, limping, toward the kitchen door with Wasaweg's diary tucked under one arm. It was clear that she was attempting to exit the cottage so that she could head straight for the barn.

"Where the hell do you think you're going?" Justin demanded.

"You can't stop me. They're *my* jewels—*mine*," she hissed.

Sarah sprang up and raced to the fireplace, and grabbed the barn key from the mantelpiece. "My mom and I are the sole custodians of this estate. The barn remains locked. No one enters it without my permission." She threw the key into the flames.

Angela returned to the table and sat down. "The fire will die down. I'll rake the key out of the ashes. Or I'll get a court order and break down your barn door. You can't stop me. De Beaumont's jewels belong to me."

"No, no! You listen to me! Those Crown Jewels are stolen goods. An innocent man, my ancestor, Matthieu Landry, was nearly killed because Sieur Beaumont wanted to bury the truth about the theft. Bernard Beaumont knew about his father's crime. That's why he wanted no part in the treasure." Sarah took a breath. "So here's what we'll do. We wait until Deanna returns from her—" she paused, "her trip." She had realized mid-sentence that she couldn't disclose to Angela where Deanna had actually travelled. "After she gets home, we'll donate the jewels to the museum that her mother works for in Montreal. The finder's reward will be donated to the Wolastoqiyik Wahsipekuk First Nation Centre and the local archaeological society—to help restore the cracked murals inside the caves. Sounds good?" She smiled. "So who wants another croissant?" She marched to the kitchen, and, with her hand on the door, grinned mischievously at the professor. "Stay for coffee, Angela. You're family."

# NINETEEN: END OF AN ERA

*Kakoua-Nak Island, autumn 1690*

Autumn arrived; on the mainland the aspens at the forest edges were now tinged with yellow, and crops in fields and gardens were nearing the end of their season. "Time to gather the last wild fruits before the first frost," Wasaweg said one day. In that moment, Deanna realized that the English attack of 1690 that Wasaweg had recorded in her diary was imminent. Lentug and Matthieu spoke, too, of rumblings of unrest up and down the lower Saint Lawrence region. After the Lachine massacre of 1689, the summer before, Frontenac had taken revenge for all the lives lost. His retaliatory attacks had in turn spurred the English to send a fleet of ships up along the Saint Lawrence River. Led by Admiral William Phips, leader of the Massachusetts Colony, the boats were moving toward the Quebec settlement that autumn—trying to reach it before the river got covered with ice floes and froze over. Kakoua-Nak Island was one stop on the way; the English would invade any day.

It was impossible, however, to think of war on such a beautiful morning. The two young women picked fruit and dropped them into their reed baskets. The sky was clear and the blue mountains on the North Shore were clearly visible.

Deanna gave Wasaweg a sidelong look and said, "Your brother never took me to see the caves, though I asked him numerous times. Is it because he still perceives me as a foreigner even after all these years?"

Wasaweg put her basket down, looked long and hard at her. "I don't know what his reasoning was. I'll take you to the caves myself. If we go today, we should go mid-afternoon. The tide will be low then. So let's meet up later by the well on the village outskirts. If we're lucky, Lentug and Matthieu won't have returned from their canoe trip."

"Would it be all right with you if I brought a box of paints with us?"

Wasaweg gave her a puzzled look. "Of course."

They were on the rocky far shore of the island, looking out across the wide river. Deanna rolled up and knotted her long skirt in the middle, so it turned into a pair of billowing shorts. Moccasins in hand, the two women scrambled barefoot over slippery, seaweed-covered boulders, and waded through shallow pools of water. The tide was way out.

Wasaweg stopped in front of a giant natural monument that rose up near the edge of the forest, a craggy statue—a face, with eyes that seemed to gaze down, benign and protecting—a statue not made by man but carved out by wind, water, and time. "The Guardian of the caves," she said and bowed her head. "It was created over thousands of years as the Great Ice receded."

Near the foot of the statue they pushed aside some bushes that screened the entrance to the first cave and stepped inside.

The ceiling arched about ten metres above them, like a small cathedral. Deanna got goose bumps in the cold, damp air. "Room for ten to fifteen people," she said.

"Yes. The First People probably spent the summers here, arriving after the spring thaw when the ice had melted," Wasaweg explained. "They camped here or pitched wigwams on the rock terrace outside the cave—it's well above the tide level. With the backdrop of the cliff, no chance of surprise attack by enemies. A perfect summer camp." She pointed at the drawing of two people wielding spears. "See—the mural painted by the First People. They lived here hundreds and thousands of years ago. We know them through their paintings and pottery."

They moved to the second cave. Deanna found it difficult to speak. She heard a melodic humming vibration. The rhythmic sound of water dripping echoed within the quiet chamber. Or was it the resonance of the First People chanting? Time stood still.

She stopped in front of the very wall painting that she had studied when she had first entered the cave with Matt, Sarah, and Justin on the eve of Canada Day. The mural depicted children playing on the beach and a big whale in the background. "Wait." She put her hand on Wasaweg's arm. "Where's the seal?"

The woman stared at her for a moment. "You're seeing a vision?"

Deanna nodded. She pulled the paints from her bag. "I'll just add in the seal right here. You don't think they'd mind, do you?" she whispered.

"Who? The First People? I'm sure they won't mind." Wasaweg said. "Do what you need to do."

Painting from memory what she'd seen in the future, Deanna inserted the image of the seal in the lower right-hand corner of the mural. When she had finished, Wasaweg said, "It seems incomplete. Here, let me add one thing." She took the paints from Deanna and added an eight-point star just above the seal's eyes, next to a small but deep crack in the rock.

"So is it a star or is it a flower?" Deanna asked, stepping back a few paces to admire their handiwork.

"It is Wasaweg's touch." Wasaweg smiled. Her eyes glowed with excitement. "We won't sign our names. Those cave dwellers who came here long before we ever did are the true artists. If they felt no need to leave a record of their names, why should we? That is the white man's way, not ours."

"Can we enter the third cave?" asked Deanna.

"How do you know about the third cave? Only our people know this secret."

Deanna was quiet.

"You do have visions," Wasaweg repeated. "I often wonder if *you* are a vision, a spirit from some other realm, maybe from the realm of the star-fields above us. Perhaps you have come to save us from the invaders."

"I wish I could. But I'm a human being." Deanna gave her a hug.

### *Twenty Days Later*

"Back here," Lentug called. "Carry the children over the rocks. We'll be safer inside the third cave."

One by one, they entered the last chamber. Deanna pulled Matthieu back just before he ducked under the low archway to join his family. "Don't question me." She handed him a piece of charcoal. "Write the English version of your name, and include the year—Matthew 1690—underneath the picture of the seal. I'm begging you to do this. It means the world to me. Do it for me and our friendship. A parting gift …"

"If it makes you feel any better on this dark day …" He shot her a wry smile and scrawled *Matthew—1690.*

They squished into the last cave where the children huddled and shivered from cold and fear.

"There are small openings at the back of the cave where smoke can get out and air can get in," Lentug said. "I think it's safe to light a small fire. The soldiers won't detect it; this cave is too far back." He knelt down and piled up small pieces of driftwood. The children lay down in their parents' laps, and the elders sat with their backs against the cave wall for support.

"We've got enough food for a few days," Wasaweg said cheerfully. "And look, Diane brought our paints." She held them up to show to her children.

"Actually, I forgot the paints last month when I came here with you—." She stopped speaking as soon as she saw the look in Lentug's eyes. He stared at her.

"You entered the sacred caves without my permission?"

Wasaweg put a hand on his arm. "Peace, brother. You're the leader and healer in the family, but the right to visit these caves belongs to me, as well. Diane accompanied me as my companion."

Lentug shrugged. "No matter. I'm sorry I raised my voice. We'll leave the island soon enough—after the

English stop blasting their guns and cannons. No member of our community will see these caves for a long time. I'm glad you got to see them under peaceful circumstances."

# TWENTY: SACRIFICE

"You take my place," Deanna was saying to Matthieu. "I'll be fine. Send someone back for me." Everyone was in the boat except for Matthieu and Deanna, and Lentug, who had already begun swimming.

"No, I insist."

"Hurry up! Wasaweg yelled from the canoe. "No time. The soldiers could return to the island any time."

At Matthieu's insistence, Deanna found herself next to Émilie in the canoe, with Matthis and Isabelle in her lap and Bellevue curled up in a basket at their feet. They hadn't been able to catch the other cats and kittens. Deanna reassured Émilie: "English people adore their pet cats and dogs. At least they'll treat the animals decently. Anyway, the grown-up cats have already learned to fend for themselves. They'll teach their young."

Wasaweg's mother and father were in front, and Wasaweg knelt in the stern, holding her paddle, all set to steer the canoe across the water to the mainland.

Deanna shot one last look at her brother. *Will I ever see you alive again?* She wondered.

"I'll see you tonight," Matthieu leaned over and kissed Wasaweg, a long, loving kiss. "I love you." He hugged Matthis and kissed Isabelle on the forehead.

"Papa, Papa! Don't forget us even for a moment. Swim like a seal! We love you!"

The wind and current were in their favour and they had made good headway, when Deanna turned around and asked Wasaweg to stop the canoe. "I'm queasy. I think I'm going to throw up."

"Can't you manage a little longer?" asked Émilie.

"No. I can't wait."

Wasaweg stopped paddling and they drifted. "Feel better? Ready to go on now?"

Deanna leaned over and spoke to her in a low voice: "Forgive me, Wasaweg. No matter what I do, don't forget that I love you all." She stood up, jumped into the water, and started swimming rapidly back the way they had come.

Deanna found Matthieu lying on the sand not moving. She touched his hand—it was ice cold. His clothing was sopping wet, his hair plastered against his forehead. His lips were blue. The shell necklace she'd given him three nights before still clung to his neck. *He has drowned,* she thought. *So much for going back in time and changing history. He drowned.* Tears streamed down her face. Anger replaced grief. *Damn! Let me at least try!* She pressed on his ribs; she had learned CPR one summer when she worked as a lifeguard. Nothing worked. Nothing could be done. In desperation and grief, she pulled out some strands of her hair and wound it around the seashell hanging from her brother's neck. *At least I can offer a part of myself when I lay him to rest,* she thought. She placed her head against his chest and lay there, too exhausted and hopeless to even cry.

Suddenly, he rolled over and coughed up streams of water. Colour rushed back into his face. He sat up and clasped the shell necklace around his neck. "What am I doing here?"

"Diane? Matthieu? Diane, *êtes-vous là?*" (Are you there?) Lentug shouted.

"Quick—this way!" She grabbed her brother's hands and pulled him to his feet, then tugged him toward the rocky slope that led back up to the caves. She knew Lentug would come scrambling over the rocks any minute. He hadn't detected them yet because the nearby boulders had hidden them. Wasaweg must have sent him back to the island to check on her. Within minutes, she heard the healer call out their names again as he paced the beach. But by then she and her brother were ensconced in the second cave.

"It's my brother-in-law!" He tried to pull away but she held his arm tightly. "For God's sake, Diane, go outside. Tell him we're both alive! He sounds sick with worry. Hey! What's wrong with you? Why aren't you listening to me? This is a nightmare! I wish I would wake up."

And just as Matthieu Landry said: "I wish I would wake up," Deanna shoved him against the mural. Matthieu dissolved before her eyes. She stood by herself in the Cacouna caves—staring at the picture of the seal.

\*\*\*

Back near the guesthouse, Justin walked over to Deanna's favourite spot on the beach and sat down by the rose bushes. The seals were howling on the reef. He closed his eyes. For the first time in years, he found himself praying—for Deanna. Sometime later, he heard a rustle. He opened his eyes. A young man stood before him—a strange apparition. Justin rubbed his eyes. For a brief moment he thought it was Matt, but since he had just left him in the kitchen—Matt was helping Sarah bake bread—he knew that was impossible. Also, this man's hair was much longer. It fell down to his waist, over rustic clothing. His clothes were soaking wet. Around his neck he wore a gold chain, from which dangled a white seashell entwined with strands of dark hair. A pair of worn out moccasins hung from his left hand. Justin spotted wet footprints in the sand leading up from the water; it appeared the poor fellow had just emerged, fully dressed, from the Saint Lawrence River.

"I'm awake!" the man blurted in French.

"Okay," Justin said. *Something's off,* he thought. *Did this guy just try to end his life in the river or is he on drugs? He needs help in either case.* "Are you all right? We're at a guesthouse nearby—come with me. We can offer you a ride to the clinic if you need any medical help."

"Have you seen my wife?" The man's eyes were wild. "My children? Émilie? Diane? Where's Diane? I was just talking to her in the cave. I don't know how I got here!"

In the months since they'd begun dating, Deanna had shown Justin many photos of her brother. Suddenly it dawned on him: this man, apart from his long hair and strange clothing, looked identical to Matthew Aynsworth. Was it possible? Could he be Deanna's brother? *If this is her long lost brother,* he decided, *I'm not about to let him slip back into obscurity.* "Hey!" Justin said. "I think I know your family. Follow me."

The two men walked along the beach and climbed the dirt road up to the guesthouse. When they burst through the kitchen door, Matt was standing by the woodstove, stirring a pot of soup and chatting with Sarah.

"Hey guys—I've found Deanna's missing brother!"

Sarah took one look at Matthew, glanced at Matt, and took command of the situation. She introduced them: "Matt, meet your namesake, your ancestor Matthieu Landry. In this lifetime, he's Matthew Aynsworth—Deanna's missing brother. Matthew, meet Matt Landry—your doppelganger from Cacouna village."

Matt stared at Matthew. Both young men were lost for words.

"I don't understand any of this," said Justin, "but I think that you guys had better get Matthew up to speed about who he is in this century. Convince him quickly. Now it's his sister—my girlfriend—who's missing. I think he was just with her, but in another time, and in that lifetime he calls her 'Diane,' not 'Deanna.' This is way beyond me. Can't deal with it. Sorry." He abruptly left all three in the kitchen and climbed to the loft. He flopped down on their bed. Deanna's perfume still lingered on the pillow case on her side of the mattress. Matthew was back, she was not.

Early the next morning, Sarah grabbed the kettle from the woodstove before it started whistling. Everyone else was still asleep. She had heard the doppelgangers talking all night in low voices in the living room. Both slept now—Matt on the pullout sofa near the fireplace, and Matthew on the rug, where he insisted he would be more comfortable. *I guess Matthew can't relate to the modern conveniences of the twenty-first century*, she thought. She crept out of the cottage on her tiptoes with her mug of Earl Grey tea in hand. She wanted to drink it on the barn stoop and think.

Justin joined her in the kitchen an hour later. "No breakfast for me. My stomach's in knots."

"I get it. Did you get any sleep?"

"No. You?" Just then, Matthew walked into the kitchen from the living room, Matt at his heels.

Justin faced the two men. Apart from their different hairstyles and clothing, they were almost mirror images of each other. "Do you need to use my cell phone to call your parents, Matthew?"

"No. Wasaweg and my children are my family. Please," he pleaded, "tell me how I can return to them. I wish I had never befriended the woman who pushed me against the mural in the cave. It's the last thing I remember before I woke up on the beach in front of you."

Justin and Sarah glanced at each other. "That woman," Justin said, "happens to be my girlfriend. You'll do well to remember she's your sister. As Matt surely must have explained to you, she went back in time to save your life."

Matthew needed fresh air. He felt claustrophobic in the cottage. The only person he felt comfortable with was Matt. All those other people, Sarah, Pierre, and Justin, kept asking questions about his life in New

France, asserting their opinions about what to do now that he was back. He pulled on some jeans and a T-shirt Justin had lent him and slipped out the front door, moving barefoot across the grass. It was still damp from the night. He wandered down to the edge of the cliff and sat in the gazebo. Sarah told him that Wasaweg had spent most of her waking hours at the lookout. She had prayed for his—her husband's—return. They had never found his body, but she had never given up hoping that she would see him again.

After a couple of hours had passed, he felt hungry and started walking back to the cottage. The smoke from the kitchen woodstove and the aroma of the mid-day meal simmering on the stove filled the air and wafted over to him. The sound of human voices and laughter from within the cottage were comforting, but he wasn't ready to join people yet. He stopped outside by the glacial rock—the glacial rock! He climbed up and sat crossed-legged. The necklace that Diane had given him that moonlit evening—the evening the sacred stone was moved from Kakoua-Nak Island—felt heavy, so heavy around his neck. He hadn't known that she was his sister in this life.

Now he began remembering both lifetimes simultaneously. Images flashed before his mind's eye, going back and forth in time: he saw Matthis as a newborn, Isabelle's first steps, his wedding night with Wasaweg. He saw his parents' proud faces when he graduated from high school, he remembered his prom, he remembered travelling with Deanna and his mother to Paris and visiting the Louvre Museum. Two film reels ran parallel inside his mind. Finally, the reels stopped.

He breathed the Cacouna air deeply. The time had come to give up the past. He unclasped the gold chain and placed it carefully on the glacial rock that symbolized protection of Wasaweg's people. It seemed like the only fitting place to offer it. The moment the white shell clinked on the rock, he became aware of a presence.

"Matthew!"

He turned and saw Deanna standing right behind him on the grass next to the rock.

\*\*\*

A hard rain pounded the tin roof. Deanna lay in Justin's arms. She had gone to bed early and slept soundly, lulled by the rhythmic, ancient sound of the elements merging—sky to rain, rain to earth, sky to rain, rain to earth. Her brother was back now. All was right with her world. Even the lost Crown Jewels were ready to be shipped to the Montreal Museum of Fine Arts as soon as she and Matthew got back to Montreal and could arrange with their mother for a museum official to transport them. She and Matthew had just a couple of days left in Cacouna in which to acclimatize from their time travels. She was doing well, because she had wanted to come home. He, however, would barely speak to her. He was angry that she had been the catalyst for his return. But at least she had got him back. And now they needed to come up with a plausible story to tell their parents in Montreal about where he'd been and how his sister had found him.

Matt, meanwhile, had gone to his home in the village to get more clothes for Matthew. When he returned to the cottage, he drew Matthew aside. They spoke in private for hours.

Around ten that night, Sarah heard the sound of Matt's car leaving the driveway. She left her bedroom and saw Matthew in the rocking chair in front of the fireplace. He was wearing Matt's black jeans and sweatshirt with *Les Canadiens* hockey team's logo on it. She did a double take. He looked identical to Matt; the only difference was that Matthew's dark hair hung down his back in a long braid. They were alone in the living room. Justin and Deanna had retired upstairs to the loft.

"Everything okay, Matthew?"
"I'm assimilating some news Matt told me."
"Oh?"
"You know he drove to the village to pick up some clothes for me."
"Yes. Good fit! Looking great, Matthew!"
"At his house, he showed my photograph to his mom, Danielle."
"Yah?"
"And she burst into tears."
"That's odd. Perhaps she felt bad for what you had to go through."
"No one should feel bad for what I got to live out on Cacouna Island. I'd say it was the experience of a lifetime, but that's a bit too much irony, isn't it?" He gave a wry grin. "Did Deanna ever tell you that I was adopted?"
"Actually, she did mention to me that you guys had accidentally discovered the adoption papers in your dad's study two days before you went missing.

Afterward, your adoptive parents felt guilty that they had never told you and that you had to find out that way. They thought it factored into why you left. Deanna didn't tell them about the incident with the painting in the museum."

"The incident. Ha!" He gave her a pointed stare. "Do you think it's a coincidence that Matt and I look identical?"

"Are you saying you're related to Matt? Could that be why Danielle got emotional? But Matt has no relatives in Montreal. He's Danielle Landry's only son. His dad died in a car accident before Matt was born. Danielle never remarried."

"I grew up in Westmount, but I'm Matt's twin brother. I just found out I'm from Cacouna."

Sarah stirred the honey into her tea and absorbed his statement. It made sense. It made so much sense. "Matt never told me he had a twin."

"He didn't know. His mom never told him until today when he showed her my photograph. She's suffered a lot. I guess she didn't want him to go through all that pain she went through."

"Separated twins usually sense something is missing in their lives."

"I don't know about Matt, but I know I did. I never fit in. No one hinted that I'd been adopted. In my gut, I knew I wanted something different from what my adoptive family had cut out for me. My Montreal parents will always be my parents, don't get me wrong. But I can't wait to meet Matt's mother … " His face turned red. "My birth mother … I want to get to know my Cacouna family, support them in some way. I could move down here, help my brother with his work. And I want to help restore and protect the river—especially the belugas and seals."

Sarah looked at Matthew. "It's mind-blowing. Even the way you speak is similar to Matt. I'm so glad for you both. And especially for Danielle. What a burden she has had to carry alone her whole life! She's such a sweet lady. I only met her a few times, but I loved her. Hey, Matthew! Do you realize that you and I are distant relatives?"

"I did not know that." He got up and hugged her.

"Very distant," she added hastily. "Not like cousins or anything."

"I get it. Matt told me you guys are in a relationship. Happy for you."

"Have either you or Deanna phoned your parents yet?"

"No. We can't tell them what happened, at least nothing about the time travel. Deanna's got a real good imagination. I've left it to her to figure out what to say. In a couple of days, Matt's going to give us a lift to the Rivière-du-Loup bus station. We'll reach Montreal by evening. But tomorrow morning first thing he's driving me over to his home. I'll meet my birth mother, Danielle, in the village."

"Wow." She gave him a penetrating look. "But something's still wrong. What is it, Matthew?"

He sat quietly for several minutes. Sarah discretely retreated to make a fresh pot of tea for them. When she returned, he blurted, "Look, don't get me wrong. I'm real glad to find out about my roots and get this chance to meet my birth mother and twin brother.

But I feel confused and off kilter. I can't stop thinking that if Deanna hadn't tried to save me, if she hadn't gone back in time and visited Cacouna Island, we would have had enough room in the canoe for my whole family—the family Wasaweg and I created together. I would have crossed over to the mainland with my wife and children and grown old with my people."

"*What ifs* and *would haves* are a killjoy, Matthew. Why not be grateful? Your sister undertook huge risks. She could have lost her life! She knew time travel was the only way to get you back. You're back with us now; I think it means you weren't meant to stay in New France forever. And I think you'll go nuts if you try to figure it all out."

"You're probably right." He chuckled. "I should go to bed. Got a big day tomorrow. Going to meet my birth mother and then phone my parents in Montreal and say I'm coming home."

## TWENTY-ONE: TIME STOOD STILL

At six-thirty the next morning, Deanna left Justin sleeping in the loft and crept quietly downstairs. Through a crack in the wooden door to the kitchen, she could see Sarah sitting in front of the woodstove; she was sipping tea from her father's antique china mug, her laptop on a small table beside her. Deanna knew she was working on her latest short story, *Return to Cacouna*, and hoped to finish it before anyone woke up. After that, she would prepare a hearty breakfast for the guests who had become more than friends—they were family now.

Deanna moved quietly. She didn't want to disturb the writer in the kitchen or her brother Matthew, asleep in the spare bedroom beside Sarah's room. Matt was back in Cacouna village; he had said he'd come over at ten in the morning to take Matthew to meet Danielle, his birth mother.

When Deanna had learned the news that Matt and Matthew were twins, she had felt happy for her brother. But Matthew was still acting strangely—he had hardly spoken a word to her. Was he still so angry that she had resuscitated him and brought him back to the twenty-first century? Surely he knew the alternative—drowning off Cacouna Island in 1690 while his family crossed to the mainland without him.

She went online and bought tickets to Montreal. The bus departed Rivière-du-Loup on Sunday. It would be an awkward six-hour bus ride if Matthew still weren't talking to her; she hoped Justin would be able to get time off work and come along as well. Meanwhile, she had to invent a plausible explanation for her brother's disappearance. Their parents would surely ask questions.

She grabbed a wool jacket and an umbrella from the wooden peg on the back of the door to the kitchen, and slipped into her billy boots. She decided to go through the front door so as not to disturb Sarah. She snuck out and stood on the wet grass, inhaling the familiar, smoky scent of a woodstove fire on a crisp, foggy morning. The rain had stopped, but the ground was soaked. A white-throated sparrow burst into song. The bird repeated its melody: a first whistle, then others a minor third up, ending with a series of short notes. Sarah had told her that her dad, Charles, had called it the 'Canada bird' because the start of its call was similar to the opening of the Canadian national anthem.

Deanna quickly descended the dirt road. Soon her boots crunched on sand and pebbles on the beach. The river lapped by her side like a faithful companion. She kept her eyes fixed on Cacouna Island; the foghorn sounded in the distance.

She strolled over to her favourite corner of the beach. The spot was protected from the wind because there was a natural hollow among the rose bushes. The bushes themselves lined the beach almost all the way to the Wolastoqiyik Wahsipekuk First Nation Centre below Cacouna village. She plunked herself down on a sun-bleached log, kicked off her billy boots and socks, and let her toes sink into the damp, cold sand. She broke off a rose, snapping the stem where it was attached to the base of the bush. *For all the people I've ever loved—I'll love you always. Your memory won't fade.* Thorns had stabbed her finger. She dabbed away the blood. Magenta blooms and crimson blood. She thought of Émilie, Wasaweg, darling Isabelle, and little Matthis. She pictured Lentug. She remembered how he had shyly laid his hand on her arm when they had crouched by the campfire in the cave before they parted ways. He had loved her. She had seen his love in his eyes and heard it in the timbre of his voice when he had spoken to her. How ironic that the healer's heart had been wounded by unrequited love. She would never, could never, forget any of them—even though they were long gone. Time stood still.

    She listened to the soothing sound of the waves rising and falling and watched the tide inch inward to shore. She couldn't tell if an hour had passed or two or three. Finally, she pulled on her socks and boots and started to head back to the cottage.

    Halfway along the beach, Deanna halted. Who knew when she would return to Cacouna from the city? Now that her brother was back, she had to help him settle into his old life in Montreal.

    She lingered, soul tugged by the stark beauty surrounding her. She gulped deep breaths of the rich Cacouna air. Dense fog had rolled over the North Shore and veiled the mountains across the river in shifting sheets of white. The fog lightened to the far right: only Cacouna Island remained visible. Sea gulls swirled overhead, and a falcon screeched and scrambled through the sky toward some unseen goal. The hill on Cacouna Island loomed, still discernible despite the veil of clouds, and rays of light crowned the gnarled spruce trees that lined its topmost edges. The trees looked like stalwart soldiers saluting their commander, about to fade into the oncoming, rolling mist. She tore herself away and headed back, brushing past the wet rose bushes to begin the long, uphill march to join everyone in the cottage. With a final, backward glance, she spoke aloud to the ever listening river and soaring clouds. "Thank you," she said.

*\*\*\**

When Justin woke up, the other side of the bed was empty. He felt those all-too-familiar palpitations that accompanied the sudden onset of fear of loss. How fragile were these human forms, including his own body. Deanna could disappear any time. Life was just like that.

He descended the ladder from their bedroom, grabbed a coffee from the kitchen, and went out to sit by himself on the glacial rock. It had stopped raining. He reflected: *Love never dies, though bodies dissolve in time, either suddenly, by an accident, or slowly, through disease and old age. A lifetime, like marriage or friendship, is but the rising and falling of a wave in the sea. Days, weeks, years, decades—what is time? It is love that matters.* "Dear God," he closed his eyes and prayed, "If You give Deanna and me the chance to share a lifetime together, I promise we'll remember love."

He felt a gentle presence approach. Deanna had returned from the beach. She climbed up on the rock and sat beside him. Her fingers interlaced his. She smiled—with inquiring eyes—and leaned in. She whispered, "You know I never stopped loving you when I was away. For you, it was a few days. For me, years passed. But I always knew I would see you again."

He placed his hand gently on her arm, leaned over, and kissed her. "Marry me," he said.

# TWENTY-TWO: MOTHER

Danielle and Matt's house faced the old Roman Catholic church in the heart of the village, where a statue of Mother Mary clasping Baby Jesus welcomed the faithful by the parking lot. Behind the church, with its silver spires, the farmers' fields made a green and gold patchwork quilt that spread for kilometres and kilometres, to the concession roads and beyond. As the car pulled into the driveway, Matthew's heart raced. He had run a marathon and now here he was, drawing up to the finishing line, ready to meet the woman whom he did not know how to address, though she was his mother. Danielle, a petite, dark-haired First Nations woman in her early forties, stood waiting on the veranda of the small house where she and Matt lived. She quickly descended the steps and met him partway across the lawn. Her eyes brimmed. She hugged him tightly.

"My boys." She looked at Matthew and then at Matt. Her chin quivered. She smiled through her tears.

"Maman, it's all right. Come sit; collect yourself." Matt gently steered her back to the steps to the house. They sat down on the bottom step and looked up at Matthew. A minute or two passed without words.

"Why did you give me away?" Matthew blurted, breaking the silence.

"I didn't," she replied. "Someone stole you from me."

"What?" He and Matt spoke simultaneously.

"Your father had died in a car accident two months before I gave birth and his death put me in a state of shock. Then, when you were six months old, you got influenza. You ran a high fever—couldn't keep any food down. So I rushed to the nearest clinic around midnight with you in my arms. I was beside myself, almost hysterical with worry and grief. The nurse on duty put you on oxygen and an IV drip, sent me home to rest, and assured me that doctors would make you well. She told me to return in the morning. When I did, you were gone."

"How is that possible in this day and age?" Matthew asked, outraged.

Matt stood up and paced the lawn. "Many children were stolen. It's all coming out now; all the country's dirty laundry's being aired in the news these days," he said. "For years it was kept in the closet. Top secret, supposedly. I had no idea this abominable practice continued past the nineteen sixties, but I guess it still happened in rural regions of the country. If a social worker or nurse considered a parent unsuitable or unstable, the baby might be whisked off by the authorities and placed for adoption. Can you imagine! Parents had no idea what happened to their newborn. They spent every waking hour worrying about his or her fate. It's called forced adoption, but, actually, it's kidnapping." Matt spoke in a matter-of-fact voice but he had a wild-eyed look. "I'm going to report this. The authorities will find and prosecute the people who did this to you, Mum, and to you," he put his hand on Matthew's shoulder.

"Unbelievable," said Matthew. "You should sue." He choked back tears. "But how can they pay us back for what we lost?" His question was rhetorical. All three were quiet.

"Well, it's in line with the legacy of the illustrious 'founding fathers' who have bridges and cities and streets named after them," said Matt bitterly. "Take Jacques Cartier. He set up crosses in places he 'discovered' and staked claims to the regions in the French king's name. Do you know what Cartier did when Chief Donnacona approached his ship?" he continued angrily. "He offered gifts to the chief, lured two of Donnacona's sons on board, and kept them captive. He kidnapped them and took them back to France and later returned to kidnap the chief, as well!" Matt's dark eyes blazed. "Poor Maman. They stole your son, my brother!"

"Your brother's quite the activist," Danielle said to Matthew with a wry grin. "But tell me, were you raised in a loving family? They're good to you, your parents?"

"They are. You'll meet them soon. They had no idea I was torn from you. They'll be outraged. I didn't know anything either until now. I'm so sorry." Matthew kneeled before his birth mother and put his arms around her neck, like a young boy who had come home, then looked in her eyes. "We have our lives ahead of us. I'll get to know you and you'll get to know me …" He didn't say what lay buried in their wounded souls—that nothing would make up for the years they had lost all because a nurse in a clinic, and an inhumane system, had decided to separate an infant from his mother.

"Let's go inside, Maman." Matt offered her a hand. She walked with her two sons, one on either side, up the stairs and into the house.

Matthew had known that First Nations' lands and rights had been usurped. Their children had been sent to residential schools to suppress their culture, language, spirit. Now he had learned that even babies had been kidnapped and taken from their parents—and he was one of them. The government was making efforts to rectify mistakes incurred long ago and was doing more than most countries where similar atrocities had been committed against indigenous people. Compensation was being offered. But you could not compensate a family after it has been destroyed.

"How was your meeting with Danielle?" Justin asked when Matthew entered the kitchen late that night.

"Beyond words. After talking and talking for hours, in the end, we three just sat around her kitchen table and played cards. It seemed like the most normal and the easiest thing to do. She's a sensitive person who has endured a lot. But she's got a wonderful sense of humour, and, to my surprise, she made me laugh so much. I really like her."

"Your adoptive parents called you 'Matthew' and Danielle named your brother 'Matt,'" Justin was saying. "That's an interesting coincidence. Did Danielle tell you your original name?"

"It was Paul. Paul Landry. Matt was born a few minutes before I was, so he was the oldest. So he was named after Matthieu Landry—according to the Landry tradition. The whole thing is surreal. I look at my brother and now know that he is both my twin in this life and my descendent, from when I was Matthieu Landry. How crazy is that?"

"Pretty crazy."

"Anyway, I'm not going to switch back to Paul."

"It'll be confusing when you and Matt are together."

He laughed. "The whole thing is bewildering! Anyway, I don't want my adoptive parents to feel that I've rejected them."

"True. They're still your parents."

"Of course! I'm very attached to them. It's just that I never fit in with their politics and society. Now that I remember my life with Wasaweg on Cacouna Island, I'm even more at a loss. It's as if I've been ejected from my only real home. I don't know how I'll manage back in the city."

"You're family now to Matt, and in a way to Sarah, too. I'm sure this won't be your last trip to Cacouna." Justin gave Matthew a quick hug and stood up.

"You're going out?"

"I'm going to lie in the hammock and stargaze. We never see the stars shine this brightly in Montreal."

"So you're coming with us on the bus? That's good. It'll be easier for Deanna if you sit beside her on the bus rather than me. We haven't really been able to talk."

"I understand," Justin nodded. "Yes, I'm coming with you." He stepped outside.

Matthew pushed open the door to the living room. A fire roared in the hearth. Deanna sat in a rocking chair, talking to Sarah. They both glanced up, but he walked past them to his bedroom next to Sarah's and shut the door without saying a word.

# TWENTY-THREE: UNVEILED TREASURES

"So, Sarah, you want me to ask my mum to send some Museum officials to pack up the jewels? Can I sneak a peek at them first? They're in the barn?" asked Deanna.

"Yes. And sure, we can get them out of the barn wall so you can see them. That's where Wasaweg hid them at her son-in-law's bidding. Do you know we had to practically physically remove Angela from the premises the other day? She wanted to break down the barn door and grab the jewels, can you believe it!"

"Who's Angela?"

"Oh, I forgot you were away when it happened. Professor Angela Jones," Sarah said. "It's a long story. Just don't bring Angela's name up to Pierre. He's still nuts about her, despite everything. Totally head over heels in love! And she's going to break his heart. She's a ruthless manipulator. Anyway, we managed to stop her; we had to threaten to call the police. It was quite a scene. She hasn't been back since, thank goodness."

Matt brought the crowbar from the trunk of his car. He tapped on the barn wall until he found a spot that sounded hollow. "This must be it," he said. He handed the crowbar to Sarah. "You do the honours."

She pried away the wooden boards easily, revealing a space behind the wood panels, containing a cloth-wrapped box. She removed the musty wrapping; inside was a small metal box with initials embossed on the lid: "C.B.," it said, in curving script—Charles de

Beaumont. She opened the lid and stared. There were the French king's lost jewels: three diamonds, a ruby, and an emerald. There was a moment of silence.

"Satisfied?" Sarah asked Deanna.

"I guess so. I was just curious. Well, at least now many people will get the benefit of seeing them in a museum. Probably in France. They belong there, of course. Speaking of works of art, what about Wasaweg's weaving? Do you still want to keep it hidden in the barn?"

"You're right," Sarah said. "Parts of the barn roof could be torn off by the next blizzard or collapse with the weight of the snow, and everything stored here would be ruined. It's time to bring Wasaweg's creation into the main house where it belongs. No more secrets."

Deanna and Matthew, together with Justin, Matt and Sarah, had one last mission before the departure for Montreal—to visit Ann Godridge. On their last evening together, the group arrived at her place at sunset. Red and gold streaks deepened across the sky with the approaching nightfall. Ann was sitting in a rocking chair on her porch and rose to greet them. She gave Matthew a long, hard look and said to Deanna, "So your brother came home at last. I knew he would."

Matt, who had been parking the car, bounded up the stairs.

"Ah, I recognize you!" Ann said to him. "What a fabulous bonfire party you hosted on Saint Jean Baptiste day." She glanced from Matt to Matthew and smiled. "I see it's a happy ending. Not only has Deanna's brother returned, you, too, have found your lost companion—

your twin. You can see it in their eyes," she said to Deanna. "They've loved each other for ages. It's why they came on earth together this time as twins."

"I don't understand," Deanna said.

"Let me tell you a little story. You're a bright girl; you'll catch the meaning between the lines. Before my husband passed away two years ago, we renewed our wedding vows. I know it sounds strange, but he made a pledge and asked a promise of me."

"What did he ask you?"

"To remain happy and never believe that who he is, his existence, got snuffed out just because the shell or outer form was discarded when his body got too worn out by age. He said I should remember that what we call dying is like when we change old clothes after they've outlived their use."

"And could you be happy, despite missing him?" Deanna asked.

"It's a rhetorical question, isn't it, dear? You see me. These are laughing wrinkles. Not a day goes by that I don't feel George's presence. Of course I miss him as much as I love him. But we're never separate. He's with me when I walk on the beach, sit on the porch, and gaze at the blue mountains across the river. I know he'll be with me when the sun sets in all its glory."

"What did he promise you?" Justin asked.

"To meet me again. That has given me great hope. Of course, we might not be husband and wife. We might even be reincarnated as twins." Her eyes twinkled. "Love takes many forms, but its essence doesn't change. You understand, don't you, Deanna. We both have read Wasaweg's diary."

Deanna grew quiet. For the remainder of the visit on Ann's porch, she kept glancing from Matt to Matthew. First she had discovered that Matthew Aynsworth had been Matthieu Landry, a sea captain, in an earlier lifetime. Then they had learned that in this life, Matt, Danielle Landry's son, was Matthew's twin brother. Now another mystery revealed itself through Ann's words, as it dawned on Deanna that Matt had been, three centuries earlier, none other than Wasaweg—Matthieu Landry's soul mate on Cacouna.

"Matthieu's my soul mate," Wasaweg had written in her journal. "He will be with me always."

What closer connection could one have than to be born as twins?

# TWENTY-FOUR: REBIRTH

Professor Angela Jones had unexpectedly quit her work at the dig and had returned to Montreal without saying goodbye to the archaeological team. Only Justin knew why. The new supervisor was far more easygoing and had given him a week off to go to Montreal when he explained that his fiancée's brother had just been found alive. Everyone in Quebec had heard of Matthew Aynsworth's disappearance. The Right Honourable Joe Aynsworth was a prominent politician and the tragedy had made headlines. A buzz had ensued among the residents of Cacouna village as news spread that the missing son had been found right here in Cacouna. It was said he had suffered traumatic shock and amnesia and had been living for twelve months, unbeknownst to them, in an abandoned residence on Cacouna Island. They wondered how he had survived. Some said he must have trapped animals and birds. Others said they had detected smoke on the island in the winter time and had wondered about it. Stories abounded.

Justin knew Deanna needed moral support as she prepared to tell her parents the story that she and Sarah had concocted. She would say that Justin had run into her amnesiac brother on the beach and had recognized him from photographs. She would remind them that Matthew had discovered he was adopted (which was true; he had found this out just before he disappeared from the museum), and say that he had taken off to discover his roots and had ended up in Cacouna, where

Danielle and Matt lived. It was not such a farfetched story.

Justin wondered how long it would take for Deanna to blurt to her parents that he had proposed marriage and she had accepted. He guessed what her dad would say. That they were far too young to think of marriage. Justin hoped that his having recognized Matthew on the beach would earn him some points. Mr. Aynsworth, in the joy of seeing his lost son, might drop his doubts and embrace Justin as a future son-in-law.

"We'll tell your parents it's a three-year engagement," he whispered to Deanna.

"Works for me," she said.

Matthew sat by himself on the bus. Deanna and Justin were across the aisle, whispering. Deanna leaned over to her brother. "Sandwich?"

"Nah. Not hungry."

"We're going to sit up front for a bit. I can see two empty seats behind the driver," Justin said. "Is that okay with you?"

"Fine," Matthew grunted.

Matthew watched the scenery whiz by as the bus barreled toward Quebec City. He glimpsed a campsite and an *auberge*—a small hotel—flit by the window. A stretch of forest hid the river for five long minutes until the grey-blue sheen of the Saint Lawrence River reappeared. The river spread like an elongated mirror beside him, reflecting myriad heavenly clouds. Like dancing deities coming to bid adieu, the clouds descended to earth alongside the trees to the right of the

Trans-Canada highway. No simile or metaphor would adequately express their mysterious beauty. He had never seen nor would he ever see again such clouds. Why was it that when something was truly striking, people often said, "Ah, it's like a painting"? He had never before understood the creative intelligence behind the force of Creation. For here was the original art form—Pure Nature—drenching his vision with beauty even as the bus drove on and the scenes flew by. He could no longer say the clouds were shapes wherein figures appeared or that he was projecting his imagination onto them; rather, the clouds were the very imagination of God, the Great Spirit. They shifted around in the unmoved sky to create, undo, dissolve, make anew, a new form, another shape ... And the real joy was, these clouds would never be replicated, could never be imitated. You could not grasp or describe them. A painting could capture the image, yes, perhaps even convey their movement, but the spirit that was awakened in his consciousness as he gazed out could never be described—it could only be experienced. The clouds were living entities. They were the reality; we on Earth were the shadows.

Then, one last glance at the river, the mountains behind, and it was all swallowed up. He shut his eyes. He couldn't hold on to it anymore. Soon it would fade like the memory of Wasaweg's people who had become his people. The feeling in his heart was like veins bursting with blood and tears and the setting sun's rays. Cacouna was his Mother and Matthew was an infant being pulled away from her ... He sank his head into his hands. How could he live in the modern world? He had survived in the wild forest with Wasaweg and Lentug by his side under the care of the Great Spirit. He'd watched his children, Isabelle and Matthis, arrive on Earth and grow. He'd seen firsthand the First Nations people dwelling on the sacred land, hiding from the French and the English who broke their treaties with every footfall. How could he return to Montreal? University?

Hours later, Matthew watched the scenes pass before him as the bus approached the suburbs of Montreal. The farmland and wooded areas had been swallowed up by grey and white factories, long metallic shopping complexes, brick row houses. None of the buildings in the industrial area on the outskirts of the city had any real charm. He saw one car lot filled with small cars, and, for an instant, perceived them as if they were a cluster of aliens camping out, on the edge of the road, waiting to invade the country. The foreigners' asphalt highway cut through pastures and farms and people's hearts and souls.

He remembered the paths of the Mi'gmaq, the silent sound of moccasins treading lightly in the light-filled forest. The memory of shots sounding out ricocheted through his conflicted thoughts. Oh how his heart had pounded as he had raced alongside Wasaweg, with Isabelle and little Matthis in his arms, pelting toward the sacred caves for refuge! The white men had invaded their sanctuary. How brazen the foreigners had been. They claimed land and believed it theirs, assumed they had discovered and owned it. He had lived the best of times with Wasaweg on Cacouna Island. Who knew what troubles she and the children had had to endure after he disappeared from their lives? He wished he could have been there to protect them. He wished he could go back one last time, manage to swim across the river and start a new life with Wasaweg. But could Fate be undone? Could anyone have stopped his wife from loving him or Deanna from searching for him after he had gone missing? He knew there was nothing he could do to go back in time, yet still his mind whispered: *Let me out of this modern abysmal greyness. Let me return to Wasaweg's Cacouna Island.*

A mysterious consolation calmed his heart, knowing that Matt Landry lived in modern day Cacouna and campaigned for indigenous rights while working at the Wolastoqiyik Wahsipekuk First Nation Centre. And Sarah would protect Wasaweg's cottage by the ancient glacial stone. She had applied for the cottage and barn—by far the oldest buildings in the area—to be designated as heritage buildings; they deserved that at the very least.

He would return to Cacouna in the autumn, he decided. He had the inheritance his grandmother had left him in the Aynsworth trust fund—that would help him with his plans. He'd return to Cacouna and put all his energy into helping Matt, Sarah, and his birth mother Danielle. With them, he could bear being in the twenty-first century. Certainly his sister also seemed to have fallen in love with the region, and he was sure he would be able to convince his adoptive parents to visit as well.

He hoped that by returning to Cacouna, he could begin to dream again.

\*\*\*

The cottage was curiously quiet. Matt had left to go back to his home in the village to collect a change of clothes and also pick some Swiss chard and snow peas from his garden for the meal he and Sarah would cook together that night. She'd invited him to stay over for the weekend. *We should invite Pierre for dinner,* she thought. *Poor guy. He's getting over waking up to the realization that he just got duped, used, and dumped by an expert manipulator. The professor took off as soon as she realized she couldn't get her hands on the hidden Crown Jewels. Let's hope Angela Jones stays buried in her books and far, far away from Cacouna.* Sarah chuckled to herself and went outside to stand on the porch below the awning of the sloping tin roof. *Almost anything is possible in Cacouna. People have been cured here, people have fallen in love here and gotten married in the small church.* She thought about her new-found friends. She knew they would become part of Cacouna too. She found herself moving across the lawn, past the gnarled old apple trees, past the flowers her father had planted, and past the orange tiger lilies, perennials, his great-grandfather had planted before him. The hammock swung empty in the wind. *Well, they come and go,* she thought. *Who knows who next will walk in through the kitchen door or find themselves sitting on the glacial stone in the garden?*

She kept walking. Down the road to the beach, and then along the wild rose bushes to sit by the water. Sarah had drawn on her dreams and on her experiences of Cacouna while writing her stories, but today as she glimpsed the mountains across the river, she saw that the very landscape had been enhanced by her stories—as if the characters had actually inhabited those places ... Deanna had pointed out the rock that Matthieu Landry had called "Mermaid Rock." There Wasaweg had sat. She must have appeared to her husband as beautiful as a mermaid. Now that ordinary rock on the beach was lined with layer upon layer of history and mythology. Who could know what was real and what was surreal, more real? The briny scent of the river drew Sarah back into the present—the seaweed-strewn sand, the wide river, two ducks just offshore, the distant mountains. The Cacouna air was like champagne, as they said, so rich, it made one feel intoxicated.

*Yes,* she mused, *it was the right decision to have kept the cottage and opened it to guests. Daddy would be proud.*

# EPILOGUE: THE SILVER STARLIGHT

*1744, Cacouna, New France*

Lentug sat on the barn stoop and sipped mint tea. "More, Great Uncle?" Claire, Lentug's niece Isabelle's great-granddaughter, stood on the lawn and perched on her toes to refill his clay mug. "Thank you, Little Rabbit." He patted her on the head. The child had his sister's smile. His eyes misted over. Wasaweg had passed away five years ago at the ripe age of seventy-five. The last decades of her life had been content; she never forgot her husband, but she ceased mourning him. Then scarlet fever brought by the white man had taken her away from Mother Earth, returning her to the Great Spirit on the summer solstice. Lentug remembered the song he had composed after she had passed on and embarked on the journey forward—into the starry fields far above Earth. She had taken the spirits' road, *Skedegmujuawti,* the Milky Way, into pure space, where she dwelt now at peace. He began humming it to himself. Little Claire lay curled up on the rug beside him and he stroked her head as he sang:

> *Sun, moon, stars, the Milky Way*
> *Make a pathway for you;*
> *A door opens from Earth to the Heavens*
> *And surpasses the sky's beauty.*
> *Your presence showers golden raindrops*

*And soaks into the ground of our hearts,*
*Your presence showers golden raindrops*
*And soaks into the ground of our souls.*

*Today, on the Summer Solstice,*
*The longest day of the year,*
*With a wave of your hand,*
*You make Death stand at the door*
*And bow before you.*
*You who are before time.*
*You have the right of command*
*And sun, moon, stars, the Milky Way*
*Make a pathway for you*
*From Earth to Heaven*
*And back to Earth again.*

*Would Wasaweg return to earth in another form,* he wondered. *Will I?* It made perfect sense to him that, until all lessons had been learned, every soul would keep returning, each time being reincarnated in a different body. *When will my departure occur? Must be soon. Yes, I know this is my last autumn. For how old am I now? Eighty-one? Eighty-two?* Time seemed to have frozen. He remembered his friend Diane as if she were an interesting dream he had once had. How long since he'd seen her face, all those years ago when she had lived with them on the island! He had loved her, but had kept his feelings close, never revealing them to anyone, not even to his sister. His destiny in this life had been solely to protect and heal the clan. He prayed that he and Diane would meet again one day in the Starry Fields beyond the Sky.

Normally, Lentug was asleep by this time of the evening. Tonight was different. He had stayed up past his usual bedtime intending to watch the northern lights that flashed across the night sky as summer moved toward autumn. He glanced at the new moon rising over the hills behind the house. The vivid stars twinkled in the crisp night air. The Great Bear and Orion's Belt shone like bright silver buttons on the cloak of the evening sky. Then, to the far north, the aurora borealis began to appear, shimmering across the universe—sheets of light, bright blue, rose red—flashing lights, pure light. Little Claire had fallen asleep beside him.

His head slumped forward and he heard Claire yell to Isabelle, "Great-Grandmother, come quickly! Lentug is sleeping but not breathing!" From a great distance he saw his niece Isabelle race over, press the side of his neck for a pulse and put her hand beneath his nostrils to feel for any sign of breath, life. "I'm alive!" he shouted. They couldn't hear him. He didn't care. He felt more alive than he had in years. He felt himself soar in the sky like *Gitpu*, Great Eagle, his wing span endless. As he flew, he felt a presence to his right. It was a *Gulu'g*, a Giant Bird, flying by his side, taking him from the Earth World to the World above the Sky.

All the colours of the forest below his ascending soul had suddenly burst into life. He could see everything with total clarity; even the detailed engraving on the acorn in a squirrel's paws was clear and crisp and beautiful.

*He saw such brilliant coverings of a million trees and slowly flushing cheeks of the hills. All the dark spruce were now sprinkled with flashes of red, brown, yellow, vermillion, all so vivid, above the broad waters of the St. Lawrence River, which gleamed dark grey under the glowering clouds ... He had forgotten how wonderful the crisp cold air was in the autumn ...*

Far, far away below him, as if at the end of a white tunnel, a distant glowing figure appeared. He thought at first that it was Wasaweg, but no—it was Diane. And there she stood, his beloved—still *her,* living her life—brushing her hair in the autumnal sunlight that slanted down through the leaves near the big rock in the clearing. He could see her chatting with someone—could it be Matthieu Landry? But no, the two figures wore foreign clothing—as if belonging to a different era. Since childhood, Lentug had had dreams or prophetic visions of that other time. And he instantly recognized that the two forms he saw below were in Cacouna, but not in his time. The cottage was the same, but it was larger and had a sloping tin roof. The barn looked old, shabby, run down.

Another young woman joined the two figures—a short woman with curly brown hair and laughing dark eyes. *Oh how she resembles Isabelle when she was younger, and, even more so, Isabelle's daughter! She's opening the kitchen door for them, offering tea.*

Lentug saw a man walk out of the barn carrying Wasaweg's weaving in his arms. He heard the man call out to the woman by the kitchen, "Where should I put it, Sarah?"

"In the living room above the fireplace, Justin, where everyone can see and enjoy it."

\*\*\*

Lentug felt his spirit begin to fully separate from the body that had held him all these years. The sensation was of downy feathers falling off the back of a young eagle as it took its first flight. He felt lighter, still lighter, and, as he looked down—one last view of the glacial rock in the garden—he saw Diane and the man named Justin. The two now were sitting on the glacial rock, holding hands, not talking, just looking at the mountains across the river. Something in the man's eyes and expression reminded Lentug of himself when he was in his twenties. A sharp pang tore apart what was left of his heart. His emotions, stifled all those years ago, rose up like a giant wave and filled every pore—until the pain turned to love so great he felt it would break every atom of his body. Why had he never fully expressed this love for Diane? He felt lingering regret. Communal duties had preoccupied him, yes, but even more than that, he realized now, he had kept distant to protect himself. The one time he had tried to talk to her of his feelings, that time when they'd been trapped inside the caves for those three days, she had hinted that her attention and devotion had lain elsewhere. Clearly, she had been devoted to some other man and that was why she had decided to leave Wasaweg's family. So why should he fault himself? Their closeness was not meant to be. At least not in this lifetime.

He saw the truth with pristine eyes as his spirit soared further and further. Then with sudden awareness, it dawned on Lentug that he himself was that other man, who dwelt in another time, to whom Diane had already been committed when she arrived on Cacouna Island! He recognized the light in the man's eyes as his own vision;

strangely, and yet it seemed so right, he began envisioning his beloved through Justin's eyes. He was Justin? Yes! He was that other man. In Justin's form, he and Diane were united at last—in a different time, and in the right place—Cacouna.

*How could I have ever forgotten You, O beloved Great Spirit,* Lentug thought as his spirit parted from the old body. *I have lived a life of dreams, a life of joy and sadness, and sometimes forgotten You, who let me float, like an eagle feather from the sky, down to this blessed Earth for a little while. This time, let me remember You unceasingly in all I love and live.*

And at that very moment, he moved into the silver starlight.

**END**

# ACKNOWLEDGEMENTS

I would like to express gratitude to our dear family friend, Graeme Ross, a celebrated artist from Montreal, for his beautiful painting that is featured on the cover.

Many friends and colleagues offered me invaluable suggestions when I wrote this book. I would like to especially thank my sister for her many hours spent editing this book, and for all her excellent comments, revisions, and suggestions.

I would like to thank Danielle E. Cyr, Senior Scholar at York University & Research Associate at the Mi'gmawei Mawiomi Secretariat. She took the time to read an earlier draft of The *Cacouna Caves and the Hidden Mural*. I am most grateful for her knowledgeable comments and perspective. Thanks to her, I was introduced to Mi'gmaq artist Josh Philbrick, who read an earlier version of the manuscript and offered me his invaluable insights and suggestions. For his feedback and wisdom, I am highly appreciative. If anything needs to be amended in my representation of the Mi'gmaq, those mistakes belong entirely to me.

Yvan Roy, publisher and editor of Journal Epik, and Christine Belliveau helped me tremendously in my research into the history of Cacouna. I also found the book *Découvrir Cacouna, ses lieux dits et ses circuits* by Lynda Dionne et Georges Pelletier (published by Epik) an invaluable source of information and inspiration.

I greatly appreciate the time, documents, maps, and photos that Viateur Beaulieu shared with me, as well as his many comments and suggestions.

Charles André Nadeau also told me about the island's history and shared documents he had researched. His ancestor had come to Cacouna Island as a teenager from Belgium in 1898 and had spent a winter in "le Prado." This was an institution that several European priests had created on the island to give shelter to a dozen teenaged European orphans.

I want to remember Canadian author and filmmaker Paul Almond for his inspiration and friendship. He encouraged me to write historical fiction (this novel is historical fantasy), and even edited a few sentences here and there in this novel. He remains an influence in my life. His presence is sorely missed. It was a great privilege to know him and work with him and a joy that I was able to help him and his friend Peter Dale Scott in locating the place in Cacouna that Peter's mother, Marian Dale Scott, had portrayed in her painting "Forest Stairway."

With the permission of Joan Almond, Paul's wife, I have, in my epilogue to *The Cacouna Caves and the Hidden Mural*, quoted a few lines that Paul wrote in October 2014, which he had shared with me in a letter. Many thanks to Joan Almond for giving me permission to quote Paul's words. They are: "*He saw such brilliant coverings of a million trees and slowly flushing cheeks of the hills. All the dark spruce were now sprinkled with flashes of red, brown, yellow, vermillion, all so vivid, above the broad waters of the St. Lawrence River, which gleamed dark grey under the glowering clouds ... He had forgotten how wonderful the crisp cold air was in the autumn ..."*

In chapter four, "Wasaweg's Diary," I have drawn from—and adapted—a few paragraphs from an account of Canada's history that was provided by Joseph-Charles Taché in his literary work "Three Legends of My Country" (published in 1861).

I would like to appreciate my neighbours Bernard Dionne and Caty Sirois, and Laurette Dionne and Carolle.

Finally and foremost, I remember and appreciate my mother, Erika, my father, Charles, and my sister, Magdalena.

My father spent many summers at Cacouna. He loved the cottage near L'Anse au Persil, between Rivière-du-Loup and Cacouna village, and, in 1974, ended up getting it from his aunt. My great aunt was married to a Canadian artist who liked to portray in his paintings scenes of rural Quebec set on the North Shore.

My father spent many hours and months fixing up the cottage and barn and hoped to spend his retirement at Cacouna, but he "retired" from this earth three days before his fifty-second birthday. His funeral was held on what would have been his birthday, something unbearably sad to me, but which forced me into a lifelong search for something eternal or unchanging that transcended birth and death. In this novel, I have utilized the idea of reincarnation as a symbolic means of expressing that the soul never dies and real love never ends.

After the death of my father, my mother continued to spend many summers at the little cottage in

L'Anse au Persil. It is thanks to her that the little house continued in good condition, because she maintained it so well over so many years.

My parents first brought me to Cacouna when I was twelve weeks old. We visited Cacouna in the autumn. Frost covered the lawn and the cottage was heated by the fireplace in the living room and by the woodstove in the kitchen. All of this I know from the stories I have been told and from the picture of my mother with me in her arms as she stood next to my father and sister outside the house during the my first visit to Cacouna. Many more visits followed, and I hope more will come. It is a blessed and sacred place.

And of course I cannot forget Ludwiga, our beloved black cat who loved to climb the lone spruce that towered above the barn.

# ABOUT THE AUTHOR

The author received her Bachelor of Arts (Honours) from McGill University, where she also pursued graduate studies specializing in medieval English literature. Her Honours thesis was on the influence of German Romanticism on the Scottish author George MacDonald.

The author is a member of the Quebec Writers' Federation. She is a publicist for Canadian authors, an editor, and an English and history teacher.

Yvan Roy, editor and publisher of Journal Epik, interviewed the author in the village of Cacouna in the summer of 2017. Yvan Roy's article on *The Cacouna Caves and the Hidden Mural* was published in 2018 in French in the 300th edition of Journal Epik, a Quebec journal.

Saroja Coelho interviewed Barbara Burgess about the novel *The Cacouna Caves and the Hidden Mural* in studio in Quebec City for the CBC show "Breakaway".

*www.thecacounacaves.com*

Made in the USA
Monee, IL
22 December 2021